Poetic Justice:

The Next Chapter

Richard Greene

Prestigious Publishing, LLC
http://www.prestigiouspublishing.org

Real Life Books are published by

Prestigious Publishing, LLC
33 Ramblewood Dr.
Wilmington, De 19810

Printed in the United States of America

First Printing, 2016

ISBN-13: 978-0-692-81128-3
ISBN-10: 0692811281

This page has been left blank intentionally.

Chapter 1

The door opens and there he is... Daryl Carter. The last time Linda talked to him, she said she needed some space to think over his proposition, and she found out he was seeing someone else.

"Hey babe," says Daryl standing there. "I got the movies." He then holds them up.

"You're late," says Linda with a less than cheerful look on her face.

"I know, but they're doing construction on the main road, and they're forcing everyone into a bottle neck," says Daryl. "I know you know about it because they're doing it right outside this development."

Linda doesn't respond.

Then Daryl says, "Can I come in?"

Linda, who doesn't want to see him at all, moves out of the way, and lets him in.

Daryl walks in, and she closes the door behind him.

Once he's inside, he puts the movies and his keys on the dining room table and says, "I'm all yours tonight. No phone calls and no text messages." He holds up his phone and puts it on the table. "I told everybody," he continues, "even my mother, if it's an emergency, call 9-1-1." Then he takes his jacket off and puts it on the back of the chair at the dining room table.

He looks at Linda and goes in for a kiss and a hug. The second he gets close to her face, to kiss her on the lips, she turns her head and offers her cheek. Daryl pauses for a second, and kisses her on the cheek.

With nothing to say, and to keep things from being awkward he says, "Let's get these movies started." He grabs the movies and his phone from the table and moves them to the coffee table. Next, he takes one of the movies from the pile, loads it in the DVD player, and starts the movie.

After about fifteen minutes into the movie, Daryl pauses the movie and says, "I'll be right back. I have to use the bathroom." Then he gets up, goes to the bathroom, and confidently leaves his phone behind on the coffee table. Faced up.

While he's gone, Linda is tempted to go through his phone, but fights the urge. A moment later, his phone lights up and makes a sound. Linda looks at the phone and she sees he just got a text message. Then the message shows on the screen of the phone. Linda looks in the direction of the bathroom. Then she looks at his phone. She gets a little closer to his phone to read the text message and it says, "Don't let spending time with her take all night."

That was the last straw.

Shortly after that, Daryl leaves the bathroom and makes his way back to the living room. The second he sits on the couch next to Linda, she says, "You got a text message."

"I did," he says picking up the phone surprised.

The second he unlocks his phone and starts to read the message, Linda says, as calm and quietly as she can, "Get out."

"Linda, it's not what you think," says Daryl trying to save himself.

"Get out," says Linda rising to her feet and moving to the side of the coffee table, away from Daryl with her arms folded.

"I told her I made a mistake. And that it was over between me and her," says Daryl trying to reason with her.

"Daryl, take your shit, and get out," says Linda out loud and pissed off. Then she starts throwing his movies at him.

He starts picking up his movies and grabs his phone. Linda makes her way to the DVD player, takes out the DVD and throws it at him and says, "I can't believe I was goin' to work things out with you."

Then she goes to the front door and opens it. He steps outside the front door, upset, with all his things in his hands. He turns around and looks at her with a face of defeat.

And she continues, "But you'll never change... Not for me anyway... I'm done."

Daryl starts to give a rebuttal. Then, she slams the door in his face.

*   *   *

A few days later, Linda goes to the park and notices there are a lot of couples there. Both gay and straight.

She also sees kids playing at the playground with their parents close by. Feeling a little bit upset because she is by herself, she grabs a pen and starts writing in her journal.

> *"With each day that goes by, the more and more I'm by myself, the more and more I start to feel like I'm meant to be by myself. It seems like everyone can find happiness in their relationships but me. What's the secret? It seems like that secret has been shared with everyone but me. And what makes it bad is that it's not just the straight couples that appear to have their act together and are happy. But the gay couples seem to be in on it too. If I could just find a man who fears God the same way that I do, maybe that could be the start to finding out what the shared secret is in relationships, that people seem to find happiness in."*

She then notices a guy by himself with two kids. Linda then becomes hopeful that there could possibly be someone out there for her. The second she thinks about going over to talk to him, he's greeted by a girl who gives him a hug and starts playing with his kids.

Chapter 2

Jamal's alarm clock goes off, and he wakes up. He looks at the time and he shuts it off. Jamal then rolls out of bed and gets to his prayer rug and positions himself for prayer. Jamal then starts praying. Once he is finished praying, Jamal lights a blunt and begins to self-medicate. Once he's done self-medicating, he gets dressed.

Next, Jamal walks to his kids' room and wakes them up. "Jameir, Shayla," says Jamal. "It's time to get up. You have school today."

Fighting it, his kids slowly wake up one at a time. First Jameir wakes up and says, "Good morning, Dad." And he climbs out of bed and leaves the room.

Then Shayla wakes up. But there's no immediate greeting. "Do I have to," says Shayla.

"Yes you do Shayla," replies Jamal. "Come on and get up so you can have time to go to the bathroom and get something to eat before we leave."

Shayla hesitates at first, but then she eventually rolls out of bed and makes her way to the bathroom.

Next, they are all in the bathroom brushing their teeth. When they are done, the kids go back to their room to get dressed. Then they head to the kitchen and sit at the dinner table. Jamal pulls out a box of cereal from the cabinet and points to it. The kids reply at the same time, "No, we want Golden Grahams."

And Jamal replies, "Golden Grahams it is."

The second the kids finish their breakfast; Jamal grabs their book bags and jackets and they head out the door.

On his way to dropping the kids off at school, Jamal stops by his parents' bakery and leaves with two bags. When Jamal pulls up to his kids' school, he gets out of the car and opens the rear passenger door. He struggles with getting the bags and his kids out of the car. He then walks inside the building with a book bag in one hand and a bag of donuts in the other; almost as if he's balancing working on one hand and being a dad in the other.

Next, he makes it to his school and arrives at a parking lot. He gets out of his car and again, with his book bag in one hand and a bag full of donuts in the other. Jamal then heads to the administration building to drop off the bag of donuts. Once he's finished with that, he leaves the administration building and goes to class.

Chapter 3

Linda pulls up to the salon in her car and she sees Emily sitting on the sidewalk, by the front door. She turns off the engine and pauses for a second. She then takes a deep breath to collect herself; and then she gets out of her car, closes the car door, and approaches the building.

"I was wondering what happened to you," says Emily, standing to her feet. "I started to call your phone but you pulled up before I had a chance to."

"My bad girl," says Linda smiling, as she unlocks the door to the beauty salon. "But you won't believe what happened to me yesterday." She opens the door and they both enter. Linda puts her things in the employee area. She changes the sign on the front door from "closed" to "open." Linda then opens the register to put the beginning balance in the till, and she closes it when she's done. Next, Linda goes and jumps in Emily's chair. And as it spins, she says, "Girl, you won't believe what happened to me yesterday."

"What?" asks Emily getting her station together.

"I went on a date with this cute guy I met at the park," says Linda.

"Oh my God," says Emily surprised. "What happened to Carter?"

"Oh please girl, I got rid of him," says Linda. "I found out he was cheating on me with another girl."

"What happened?" asks Emily, giving Linda her full undivided attention.

"Well, he and I were supposed to be spending time together at my house, to work some things out," replies Linda. "And when he got up to go to the bathroom, he left his phone on the coffee table, in front of the couch we were sitting on."

"No...," says Emily

"Yes...," Linda responds. "And he wasn't even gone that long before he got a text message. So, I read it, and it said something like, 'don't spend all your time with her,' And I said, "That's it." And I broke up with him and kicked him out of my house."

"What did he have to say?" says Emily interested.

"He said, that he made a mistake and that it was over between them," Linda replied. "But you know that means he's been talking to her longer than a week. And they probably even screwed each other."

"Were you guys on a break or something?" Emily asks getting back to setting up her station.

"And that's the thing," says Linda sitting up in the chair. "He said he wanted to take things to the next level by having kids and starting a family. We already weren't seeing eye to eye on a few things. He's forgetful. His money management is awful. He's irresponsible sometimes with his affairs. And sometimes when he does things, it seems like it benefits him only. I feel like he's been leaving me out of the loop. So, I told him I needed some space and time to think about it—not break-up, and go do whatever you want to do."

"How much time did you say you needed, 'cause anything over a week, and you know it's over girl," says Emily finishing organizing her station.

"He brought this to my attention on Sunday," says Linda. "I told him to give me till the end of the week to think things over. Emily, I called him three days later, and told him to come over. And to think, I was going to fold because I figured he can change."

"Enough about Carter," says Emily. "Tell me about this date you had over the weekend."

"Weeeelll," says Linda lighting up and getting exited. "It wasn't a date, per se. I was at the park and I saw this gorgeous man there playing with two kids..."

"Here I'm thinking you about to give me some juicy details about your weekend escapade," says Emily, cutting her off and walking away.

Linda grabs Emily saying, "Nooo, nooo, just listen. He was really handsome, and he was by himself. I started to make my way over there; then Miss Blocker comes from out of nowhere and gives him a hug and starts playing with the kids. I was crushed."

"That could have been anyone," says Emily.

"I know, I know," says Linda hating to admit it. "I would have just felt stupid and embarrassed if I went over there to talk to him, and it turns out to be his wife or something."

"It's always better to know than to not know," says Emily. "I mean, the worst thing he could have possibly said is no."

"I know, but I hate being rejected," says Linda.

"I'm sure guys do too," says Emily. "And we do it to them all the time."

"I know you and John are still together," says Linda, trying to strike gold. "What's the secret? It seems like everybody knows and is in on it; and you guys are just leaving me out in the cold."

"I stopped seeing John 'cause he wanted to make a career out of being in the army, and I wasn't having it," says Emily. "I understand if you want to do your four years and leave it at that, but to keep things going on like that, I couldn't handle it."

"So other than that, were things going good for you guys?" Linda asks, probing.

"Yeah. It was cool," says Emily reflecting on it.

"So how did you make it work after two years," Linda asks, getting to the bottom of it.

"It was a year and a half but I don't think there's any secret to it," says Emily. "I didn't play games like some girls like to do. And I kept an open line of communication between us. If there was something specific I wanted, I told him. I didn't make him guess and get mad if he got it wrong. And the same went for him too."

"I don't know," says Linda thinking. "Maybe seeing that guy at the park was a sign. I was thinking about going to a bar to meet someone. But who knows. Maybe he'll come to me. Maybe our paths will cross and I just have to be ready for him. Maybe he'll walk right into my life."

Chapter 4

Jamal is walking through the hallway at "University College" on his way to class. He arrives there ten minutes early before class starts. Jamal looks at the time on his phone, and says to himself, "Ten minutes before class starts... cool. That's just enough time for me to check my email real quick." So, Jamal goes in his book bag and pulls out his laptop computer. He opens it on the desk, unlocks the screen and jumps on the school's Wi-Fi. After a few clicks, he's able to login his email account. Jamal notices he has an email from Virtex, the job he just had an interview with. But he's left confused after reading the letter. It said:

Dear Candidate,
Thank you for your expressed interest in working for Virtex. We regretfully inform you that per our

interview the other day and after careful consideration, we have determined that your qualifications do not meet the needs of the current position we are trying to fill in our IT department as a Programmer.

We will keep your application on file for 90 days should a position becomes available.

Again, thank you for your interest in working for Virtex.

Sincerely,

Jennifer Sealy
Recruiter, Human Resources
Virtex

Jamal jumps up from his chair and says, "Man! This is some BULL SH..." Before he finished that word, Jamal noticed some of the students in the class were looking at him. And before he could draw any more attention to himself, Jamal laughed it off with a fake laugh, and sat back down in his seat. He then makes a mental note to give his friend Matt a call about the job and the email he just received. Matt was Jamal's hook-up for the job. And in walks the teacher. "Class," says Mr. Brolin. "Clear your desks and get ready for a pop quiz."

*   *   *

Poetic Justice: The Next Chapter

Jamal left his school and is on his way back home. On his way back home, Jamal can't shake the sadness and depression setting in from the email he received earlier today saying he didn't get the job after he was cleared for it. So instead of dwelling on his misery, he decides to try and cheer himself up and go out to dinner and a movie. In order to do this, he needs someone to pick up the kids from school, and watch them. So, Jamal decides to see if his mom is willing to watch the kids for him for a bit.

Jamal picks up his cell phone and calls the bakery. His mother answers, "Hello. Thank you for calling the Family Bakery. This is Beverly speaking, how can I help you?"

Jamal responds, "Hey Mom, it's Jamal. Are you busy at the moment?"

"No I'm not. Why, what's up?" inquired Beverly.

"Not too much," Jamal replied. "I was wondering if you could do me a favor?"

"What's that?" Beverly asks.

A little nervous Jamal answers, "Can you pick up the kids from school today and watch them for me? I have a date."

"Sure. How long will you be gone?" says, Beverly.

"A few hours. I should be back by nine-thirty, ten o'clock. Depending on when the movie starts," says Jamal.

"Okay. I can do that. How was class today?" Beverly asks.

"It was fine. We had a pop quiz today, and I'm glad I did my homework, because that's what it was mainly on," says Jamal confidently.

"Oh Okay," says Beverly. "So you think you did pretty well?"

"I feel like I did good, but him grading the paper is totally different," says Jamal.

"That is true; however, try to make sure you give him the answer he's looking for. Sometimes *your* answer and *his* answer can be different," says Beverly.

"Yeah, you're right about that Mom," says Jamal.

"I usually am," says Jamal's mom smiling. "I'm not going to hold you. Go ahead and have fun, and I'll talk to you later."

"Ok Mom. See ya," says Jamal.

"Byyyyyeee," says his mom smiling.

*   *   *

Linda isn't having the best day either. It's been a slow day at the salon and she's looking to escape the harsh realities of life that have been giving her a hard time. So she decides to treat herself to a dinner and a movie since she can't find a man to do it for her. Linda talks to Emily and says, "Emily, do you mind closing the salon for me? Something's come up."

"Sure," says Emily. "I was just about to ask you if you were okay. You look out of it."

"I've got a lot on my mind right now. I just need some time to get myself together," says Linda. "I'll see you tomorrow."

"Okay girl. I hope you feel better," says Emily.

Linda grabs her things and heads out of the salon. With food on her mind, she is on her way to her favorite restaurant.

Chapter 5

Jamal pulls into the supermarket parking lot and looks for a parking spot. The first parking space he comes to, he loses to another driver who made it to the space just before he did. The next parking spot he comes to, an SUV starts backing up. And when the SUV is just about pulled out all the way, it goes back into the space. The SUV was just adjusting itself to the parking spot as it turns out. Feeling annoyed and somewhat defeated, Jamal drives by and looks for another parking spot. After circling the parking lot a few times, Jamal finally comes to an empty parking spot. And after looking around for takers, no one is there but him to take the spot, so he pulls in with no conviction. Jamal parks the car, puts the car's gear in "park", and shuts the car off.

Jamal then takes a deep breath and looks around. Nobody is in his immediate sight, so Jamal turns the car battery on and the radio starts playing. Jamal sets the car radio to auxiliary, turns the volume down some, and connects the iPod to the radio.

Next, he takes the partially smoked blunt from his ashtray and puts it in his mouth and grabs the lighter. Jamal slouches in the seat some, lights the blunt, and takes a deep pull. He then exhales and pushes play on the iPod. When he pushes play, the song "P.O.D." from Bone Thugs -N- Harmony starts playing. Then Jamal takes another deep breath and starts reflecting on events happening in his life.

After another pull, a lady in a satin-brown cocktail dress with fire-red hair appears in the front passenger seat; and looks at Jamal with a smile on her face. She then opens the car door and leaves after a moment of sitting in the car with Jamal.

Jamal then looks at the clock on the radio and it says 4:17. Then he turns the car battery off. He takes another pull from the blunt and puts it out in the ash-tray. Jamal opens the car door and leaves the car closing the door behind him.

Jamal floats through the parking lot, with his feet a few inches off the ground, towards the supermarket. He bypasses the shopping carts and floats through the automatic door after it opens. While inside, Jamal floats through the front of the store. And as he floats through the front, people are moving to the side, out of his way, as he floats past them. Almost, as if he's parting the Red Sea.

When Jamal gets to the candy aisle, there are people standing to the side of the aisle, lined up, as if they were awaiting his arrival. Jamal then goes to the section half-way down the aisle and grabs some Milk Duds, Peanut Chews, and some gummi bears.

Next, Jamal leaves the candy aisle and gets in line at one of the register lanes to purchase the candy. While in line, Jamal grabs the orange soda in the refrigerator to his left, and puts his items for purchase on the conveyor belt in front of him. Just as the customer in front of him is finished with his transaction and walks off, Jamal leaps forward in the air and spins horizontally, like a cork-screw, down the lane to the register. The cashier tells Jamal the total and with cash-in-hand, he places it on the counter next to the credit card reader; and continues to float by. Jamal tells the cashier to keep the change and grabs his plastic bag full of goodies. He places it on top of his stomach as he floats by, horizontally, on his back, with his hands folded behind his head.

The cashier stands idle as she watches him float down the front end of the store, and towards the automatic door. Jamal notices her watching him and he pulls out a small, square sign, on a handle, with dotted lines on the sign that reads "Bye," and waves it to her as he leaves out of the front door. Jamal's feet touch down on the ground, once he's outside, in front of the store. And he walks off to his car, and leaves the shopping center.

Next, Jamal is on his way to his favorite restaurant. When Jamal arrives, he has no problem finding parking. Once he's inside, he goes to the host at the podium and she asks, "How many are in your party."

Jamal answers, "Just one".

And the host tells him, "It'll be a five to ten-minute wait."

Jamal says, "Okay," and takes a seat on the bench just a few feet from the podium.

While Jamal is waiting, the lady in the satin-brown cocktail dress and fire-red hair walks through the door. She approaches Jamal and stands in front of him with her

Richard Greene

hand extended out. Just as she is standing there, the host walks to Jamal and says, "Sir, your table is ready." Jamal turns to her and says, " Okay," and grabs the lady's hand in front of him. He stands up, and follows them both farther inside the restaurant. The host seats him just on the outside of the bar near the entrance to the kitchen.

"Your server will be right with you in a minute," says the host smiling.

"Okay," says Jamal.

Then he turns his attention to the woman in the satin-brown cocktail dress who's sitting across from him. She opens the menu and hands it to Jamal and she points to the "Extreme Nachos and Cheese" appetizer. He sees it and looks at her and says, "Okay." Then asks, "What are you having?"

"Ma'am, what are you having," says the server to Linda. Linda responds, "I'm sorry. I can't make up my mind right now. Can you start me off with a water and lemon?"

"Sure," says the server. "I'll be right back with it."

While she is waiting for her drink, Linda pulls out a pen and her journal and starts writing.

> "Time waits for no one.
> Not even in a life or death moment,
> Where there could be a pause and a chance for a life saved,
> For the person on the other side of the gun.
> Time is our friend. Time is our enemy.
> Time could run out while we're searching for our soul mate,
> While others who have it, and happiness surrounds us,
> And our hearts filled with envy.

Time wastes as we search for what's inevitable.
And in a small moment of success,
Our excitement says it's our destiny.
While we put it to the test,
Is it fate that makes you the best for me?
As I stand here waiting, as I sit here waiting,
Time runs out, as does the energy,
Deflating.
And as I become depressed,
I'm grid-locked under this dark cloud,
Save me."

Jamal is at the movie theater, watching a movie, with the woman in the satin-brown cocktail dress and fire-red hair sitting right next to him. With his arm around her, they start reacting to the movie. And the woman in the satin-brown cocktail dress disappears.

A few rows behind him, however, is Linda sitting by herself in almost the same place as the woman in the satin-brown cocktail dress was. She's eating popcorn, drinking her soda and also reacting to the movie.

Chapter 6

The next day, Jamal's phone rings twice, and it wakes him up. A little disoriented he looks at the clock and it's says 9:30 a.m. The phone rings again. He picks up the phone, and he answers, "Hello."

"Good morning son of mine," says Beverly.

"Hey Mom... good morning," says Jamal.

"How was your night last night," asked Beverly.

"It was fine," Jamal answers.

"I hope you had fun, because someone forgot to call me," says Beverly.

"I know Mom. I just realized that," says Jamal.

"You should be fortunate that your children are well behaved," says Beverly. "I took them to school for you this morning, instead of having them work with me in the bakery."

"Did you," says Jamal.

"Yes I did," says Beverly.

"Thanks," says Jamal. "I can get them from school this afternoon. You don't have to worry about it."

"Okay," says Beverly. "Jamal, I'm calling you because we have no one to do deliveries for us today, and was wondering if you would come in and help us out."

"Yeah, I can do that," says Jamal. "What time do you want me to come in?"

"Is now okay with you?" asks Beverly smiling.

"Yeah, I can leave now," says Jamal. "Just give me a few minutes to get dressed, and I'll be on my way.

"Okay. See you soon, son," says Beverly.

"Okay Mom," says Jamal. "Bye."

Jamal hangs up the phone and rolls out of bed. He brushes his teeth, throws some work-clothes on, and heads out the door.

*   *   *

Jamal makes it to the bakery and goes inside. His mom comes out to the front of the store after she hears the doorbell go off and ends up greeting Jamal, "Hi Jamal."

"Hey Mom," says Jamal.

"Glad to see you made it," says Beverly. "You got here faster than I thought you would."

"Yeah, I just rolled out of bed and came straight over here," says Jamal.

"Good," says Beverly. "There's a delivery over here in the glass case, and it needs to go out. A-sap."

"Okay, no problem," says Jamal looking in the glass case. You mean this box right here?"

Beverly turns around and sees Jamal holding up a box and says, "If you got that from the glass case, then yeah... It should be marked."

Jamal looks at the top of the box and it's marked. It says, "Linda/Salon. Doz asst."

"Hey Mom, what happened to the delivery guy?" Jamal asked, putting the box in a plastic bag. "What, y'all let him go or something?"

"No, not yet," Beverly answers. "He just didn't show up today for some reason. We called him and everything. And we got no response."

"Wow," says Jamal surprised. "Sounds like he won't be having a job soon."

"Jamal, I almost forgot," says Beverly. "That delivery is for Linda that owns the beauty salon around the corner. Please be nice to her. We get a lot of business from her."

"I will," says Jamal without a problem.

"Oh and Jamal," says Beverly smiling. "I hear she's single."

"Oh boy, here we go," says Jamal walking off with the bag in his hand.

"All I'm saying, Jamal, is play the field a little," says Beverly, trying to sound convincing. "Who knows, you two could be good together."

"I'm fine where I'm at, Mom," says Jamal from the front door. "I don't have to come out of my pocket much when I go out now."

"That's because you're going by yourself," says Beverly with a big smile. "It doesn't cost much when you have someone with you when you go out."

"Bye Mom," says Jamal walking out the front door.

Chapter 7

Jamal goes around the corner, crosses the street, and goes up two blocks. As he approaches the salon window, he sees that it's a full house. Everyone is laughing and talking amongst themselves. Not sure on what he is about to walk into, Jamal turns his baseball cap around, facing the back, and prepares himself for what he's about to walk into. He goes to the front door of the salon, opens it, then he walks inside.

"Oh look girl. Here comes one now," says Linda finishing a client's hair. "I got this."

"No, wait," says Emily.

But Linda pays her no attention and responds with, "I'll be right back."

Oh boy. Here we go, says Jamal to himself, standing at the register.

The girls in the salon get quiet so they can hear the exchange that's about to take place.

"How can I help you?" asks Linda walking to the register. "Wait, let me guess... you want to sell me something," says Linda looking back at her friends smiling.

The girls in the salon snicker and makes a little noise. Then they start shushing each other. Then they finally get quiet before she continues.

"No, I'm here because...," Jamal starts.

"You need a job," says Linda, cutting Jamal off and glancing back at the girls before she continued. "No, wait... I got it," says Linda smiling. "You saw me through the glass window over there and you want my number, so you can 'talk' to me," Linda says, folding her arms in front of her contentedly, convinced that she's "got" him by guessing his intentions correctly.

"No," Jamal laughs. "I'm here to deliver these donuts to a Linda," says Jamal, dropping the bag on the counter.

"Oh, (looking back at her friends) so you're the delivery guy for the Family Bakery," says Linda somewhat surprised and feeling apologetic.

The girls respond in disgust and disappointment. "Told you," someone says. And then they listen in, even more now.

"Yes," Jamal says.

"What happened to the other guy?" Linda asks. But Jamal doesn't respond. He just stands there smiling.

"Oh... How much do I owe you?" says Linda casually.

"Fifteen dollars," Jamal responds.

Linda grabs her purse from her bag behind the counter. She opens it and starts to give Jamal a twenty, but then changes her mind and gives him a ten and all of her ones.

"Here's fifteen even," says Linda.

"Wow. Can't break the twenty huh," says Jamal, taking the money and counting it. "Somebody's cheap and trying to look like she got money... aaand you're short, by the way."

"Does somebody have...," Linda starts. "Never mind." She then goes into the register and pulls out a dollar.

"Here you go," says Linda. Handing Jamal the dollar. "And for your information, I don't like carrying..."

Jamal's phone rings.

"Oh, and would you look at that. Just in the nick of time," says Jamal cutting her off and picking up his cell phone.

"...around a lot of change," Linda finishes. But Jamal isn't paying her any attention.

Jamal looks at the screen and says, "I got to go. And not that it's any of your business, but, this call is about a **job**. Peace."

Jamal walks out of the salon and answers his phone call, "Hello."

"Hey Jamal... it's Matt."

"Yo, what's goin' on."

"I was just callin' to see if you're ready for your first day at work in a few days."

"First day? They gave me the can the other day in an email," says Jamal walking across the street. "I thought I didn't get the job."

"Nah bro. There must be some sort of mix up. Robert just came to me a few minutes ago and said, 'I hope your boy works out. We're starting him in a few days.' Who sent you the email?"

"Jennifer did," says Jamal as he stops walking. "The recruiter from H.R."

"Dude, look... I'm going to text you his office number. When you call, his secretary's going to answer. Just tell her you wanted to confirm your start date with Mr. Cassas. Tell her you just got the message and she may not have that information yet. She should put you through to him."

"Okay. I'll call him in a minute and see what happens."

Jamal receives a text message.

Jamal looks at the screen on his phone and says, "I just got your text."

"Okay, kool, kool. Okay bro, I got to go. I just called to give you a heads up," says Matt.

"Yeah, and it's a good thing you did Matt, thanks," says Jamal. "If I don't talk to you later, I'll see you in a few days."

"Al'ight bro. I'll talk to you," says Matt.

"Bye," says Jamal as he starts walking again.

Emily heads out of the salon and goes after Jamal. "Jamal," she yells from across the street. Jamal turns his head to see who's calling him. After he sees who it is he keeps walking. Emily crosses the street and finally catches up with him.

"Jamal, I hope you're not mad," says Emily feeling concerned.

"I'm not," says Jamal. "I just don't have time for people who try to play me out in front of a crowd like that."

"I know, I'm sorry, and I'm apologizing for her," says Emily.

Jamal doesn't respond.

"Jamal stop," says Emily as she gets in front of him. "Linda is a nice girl... give her a chance."

"I don't know," says Jamal. "It doesn't seem like she needs it from me."

"Of course she does," says Emily. "Look, all that was just play 'cause the girls was in there; and you know how we can get when we get the talking. I'm not saying you have to spend money on her..."

"What do you want me to do," says Jamal exhaling and giving in.

"The next time we order something, just show up with the order, and we can take it from there," Emily says. "If you like her, kool. That'll be what's up."

"What if I don't like her?" says Jamal.

"Well, it's her loss," says Emily casually. "No biggie. And you don't have to see her again."

"Al'ight. I can do that," says Jamal.

"Kool. I'll see you later," says Emily going back to the salon.

Jamal continues on and heads back to the bakery.

Chapter 8

The next day, The Family Bakery gets an order from the salon and Jamal is there to receive the order, fill it, and deliver it. Jamal gives himself a pep talk before he leaves for the salon, "Okay. This is it. Don't fuck it up. She's kool, and *wants*, the conversation." Jamal takes a deep breath, leaves the bakery, and walks to the salon.

On his way there, Jamal can't help but think about what happened the last time he was there. The exchange wasn't friendly at all. And it kind of turned him off.

Jamal crosses the street and approaches the salon window. As he's walking past it to the front door, he doesn't see Linda at all. Jamal opens the door, walks to the register, and is greeted by Emily. "Hey Jamal."

"What's going on," Jamal replies placing the box of donuts on the counter top, next to the register.

"Not much," says Emily. "You just missed Linda. She ran to the bank."

"Really," says Jamal. "How long you think she'll be gone for?"

"About a half-hour, 45 minutes. Somewhere in there," says Emily.

"Damn, I can't wait that long," says Jamal. "I got somewhere to be in a half hour. I came by here on my way out."

"Well, I'll let her know you came by," says Emily with a smile on her face. "Who knows, maybe I can get her to come by the bakery."

"Hopefully, but, we'll see how it works out," says Jamal leaving the salon. "I'll talk to you later."

"Okay, Bye Jamal," says Emily taking the box to the employee area.

*   *   *

Jamal walks back into the bakery and says hello to the customers. And as he walks behind the counter, he speaks to his mom who is talking with the customers.

"Hey Mom," says Jamal. "I'm on my way to orientation. I just came by to change my clothes."

"Okay my son," says Beverly grinning. "Have a good first day at work."

"I will," Jamal responded.

He then says hello to his dad, who is in the middle of decorating a cake, and walks into the office; and closes the door. A few moments later, Linda walks in and approaches the counter. She is greeted by Beverly. Beverly invites Linda to come behind the counter so she can see some of the cakes being worked on. Linda walks behind the counter and follows Beverly to the back. The second she passes by the office door, Jamal opens the office door and walks out. He proceeds to the front of the store and says, "See y'all later." Then Jamal heads out, on his way to his new job.

Chapter 9

Jamal pulls up to his new job and parks the car. Jamal gets out of the car and walks up to the front of the office building and there is Matt sitting on the bench, smoking a cigarette. He puts out his cigarette and greets Jamal, "Yo, what's good?"

"Not much," says Jamal giving him a hand shake and a half hug while he's holding his hand.

"I see you finally made it," says Matt.

"Yeah, pretty much," says Jamal excited looking at the building.

"You ready? 'cause everybody that works for this company gets paid," says Matt. "Especially when they start."

"Damn right," says Jamal excited, with a smile on his face.

"Now that's what I like to hear," says Matt. "Follow me."

Jamal walks with Matt through the lobby and to the elevator doors. While waiting for the elevator, Jamal looks around and notices that the maintenance people are hanging up new paintings in the lobby. The elevator "dings" and the elevator doors open. They both walk inside, along with two other people. One of the two other people on the elevator pushes the 3rd floor button. Matt pushes the 5th floor button and the door closes.

When the elevator door closes, it becomes dead quiet on the elevator. Jamal looks at Matt and he's on his phone not paying attention to anything. Then he looks at the two people in front of him through the reflection on the elevator wall, and one of them is a short Vietnamese girl. The other person, taller than her, is a Chinese guy. The Vietnamese girl appears shy, keeping to herself with her head down. And the Chinese guy looks like he's ready to get the day over with. The elevator finally makes it to the 3rd floor. The elevator dings, the doors open, and they both walk out of the elevator; Vietnamese girl first. Then the elevator doors close behind them and continues to the 5th floor.

On their way up, Matt says impatiently, "This elevator is fuckin slow as shit. I could watch 'The Shawshank Redemption' on my phone twice, to the end of the credits, and we'd still be in here.

Jamal laughs and Matt starts pushing the 5th floor button repeatedly saying, "Come oooon. Nobody wants to be stuck on an elevator."

Once they reach the floor, before the elevator dings, you can hear something indistinctive coming through the elevator door. The elevator dings and as soon as the door opens, the indistinctive sound was now clear. It is the atmosphere on the floor. It's alive.

Matt walks off the elevator first and turns his head to Jamal, who's right behind him, saying, "Welcome home."

They walk across the floor and once they reach the first set of cubicles on the right, Matt says pointing, "This is where my team is. I sit right here." Then he taps the cubicle wall, twice, right next to him where the cubicle wall ends. "Now I don't think they'll have you guys out in the open like me," says Matt taking off his hoodie and putting it around his chair. "I think they have you guys in a room at one of the corners on this floor."

Jamal, distracted by the flyer on the bulletin board, hanging on the cubicle says, "Y'all, I mean **we** have a conference coming up?"

"Oh you mean this," says Matt pointing to the flyer. "Yeah. They have it once a year. Then they have a company one, but, nobody goes if it's out of town."

"Whaat," says Jamal in disbelief.

"Yeah," says Matt. "I told them they're out of their fuckin mind for not wanting to go. I mean, how do you turn down free everything? I told Rob, if they ever invited me to go, I'd be there. But that has yet to happen. And speaking of the devil, let me take you to him. He's right over here."

Then Matt walks right across the floor, not too far from where they were, to Robert's office. His door is already open, and Matt knocks on his door frame, then leans on it and says, "Hey Rob. I got Jamal here for you."

Rob, focused on his computer screen, without turning around, sticks his hand out to the side and motions to Jamal to come in, and says, "Come in... have a seat." And before Matt has a chance to leave, he says, "Hey Matt, we're going to Buffalo Wild Wings after we get off... Bring your 'A' game."

Matt turns around and comes back to the doorway and says, "You got to be fuckin kiddin' me. You're the one that eats the hot wings with blue cheese on it, like you're a four-year-old."

"That's because..." says Robert turning around. And closing a book he was holding in his lap, he puts it on the desk in front of him. "I need my stomach lining. And I want to be able to taste my beer when I use it to wash my food down with it."

"Unbelievable," says Matt. "I'll talk to you later about it. I got work to do." Then he walks off.

"Welcome to the family," says Robert standing up with his hand out.

Jamal shakes his hand.

"Have a seat," says Robert. And they both sit down. "Now, did Matt give you a tour of the place yet?"

"No," says Jamal. "We came straight here once we got off the elevator."

"YOU TOOK THE EVELATOR," says Robert surprised. "You must have aged some."

"I didn't think it was too bad," says Jamal laughing a bit.

"We usually take the stairs," says Robert quietly while he starts looking around the desk for something. Then he looks on the table to his right and sees a manila folder and says, "Ah, here it is."

Next, Robert opens it to makes sure it has what he's looking for in there. And it does. Then he hands it Jamal and says, "This is a list of languages we use to write most of the software that comes out of here. Have you done any further research on the company since the last time I talked to you?"

"No, I haven't," says Jamal feeling like he should have now that he mentions it. "Was I supposed to?"

"No, not really," says Robert. "Once the word got out that we helped develop a few games for Nintendo, we started getting a lot of applicants wanting to work on the next Nintendo project. But before I let you get settled in, let me give you the full scope of what we do here and what's expected of you. Virtex is a software company that designs and programs software that helps people learn in children and adult education. The project we're currently working on, is an application that is able to determine the best way a child or adult is able to learn. We've worked with companies such as 'Leap Frog' and 'School Zone.' We even helped develop some video games, like I said before, for the Nintendo DS. With games like 'Brain Age' and 'Big Brain Academy'," he says pointing to the game cases on the table sitting against the wall behind his desk.

"We're just about finished with the program we're working on now, and we need to Beta test," says Robert. "And that's where you come into play. We want you to survey about 500 people or so, report the data, and give a presentation on your findings at the conference we have coming up."

"Is that the conference coming up in Orlando?" Jamal asks. "I saw the flyer on the bulletin board."

"Yes it is," says Robert. "Do you think you can handle that?"

"Yeah, but," Jamal laughs a little. "Why me? I mean, I'm just starting today."

"I know that," says Robert. "But you're the only one who checked 'willing to travel' on his application. I shouldn't have to pull teeth for you or anyone to go to this conference. It's in Florida for Christ's sake. Follow me, says Robert standing up from his desk. I'm going to show you where you'll be working, and introduce you to the rest of the team. Then, if he's not too busy, I'll let Matt show you around."

Chapter 10

"And since we finished this chapter ahead of schedule, I don't see a need to assign you homework over the spring break," says Mr. Brolin.

"Yesss," replied the class softly.

"Enjoy your spring break," says Mr. Brolin as students from neighboring classes, leave their classes, and fill the hallway. "And I'll see you when you get back. Class dismissed."

The students in the class start to get up and pack their things and leave the class.

"Oh, and by the way," says Mr. Brolin, trying to talk over the small commotion of students talking to each other as they leave the class. "If you want to get a head start on some classwork and homework, read chapter 13 and answer the 'Quick Study' questions at the end of the chapter. If you turn in the assignment early, I'll give you extra credit."

Jamal quickly writes down the extra credit assignment, and with the rest of the class, he leaves as well. Jamal then navigates the hallways on his way to the computer lab. Once he gets to the computer lab, he finds an open computer, and occupies it. He then gets on the internet and logs on to "Blackboard" to turn in some homework assignments. About a half an hour after being there, his friend from class, "Kenny," walks in. He sees Jamal, and goes to say, "What's up?" to him.

"Yo Jamal, what's good?" asks Kenny.

Jamal turns around in his seat and says smiling, "Just the man I wanted to see. What's goin' on?" Then he gives Kenny a handshake.

"Not much," says Kenny. "I'm about to take this test real quick before my next class. What you got goin' on?"

"Not too much," says Jamal. "I'm just turning in some work before I get out of here. You got plans for spring break?"

"I'm supposed to be getting up with this girl I know and go to the movies or something," says Kenny. "But she ain't been hittin' me back. So I don't know for sure."

"Good," says Jamal. "While she's deciding to get her priorities together, you can tell her you'll be out of town. Remember that job I was tellin' you about that I got?"

"Yeah," says Kenny sitting down in a chair next to Jamal and taking off his book bag.

"Well, I started the other day and they want me to give a presentation next week in Orlando, Florida, at some convention they have every year," says Jamal.

"Damn, that's good shit," says Kenny.

"I know," says Jamal.

"You think there'll be girls there?" says Kenny.

"I'm not sure," says Jamal. "The conference, from my understanding, is only supposed to be for a day or two. And that doesn't give us enough time to do anything."

"You're right," says Kenny somewhat defeated.

"Whoa, I got an idea," says Jamal with a smile on his face.

"What's that?" Kenny responds.

"What if we bring some girls with us," says Jamal in his "ah ha" moment. "That could make the trip better on the ride to and from. Plus, that'll give me some extra help if I need it."

"Well, who could we bring?" says Kenny out of ideas. "I doubt that girl I was tellin' you about would be game."

"Well it's still early. Don't count her out yet. And there's these girls I know that work at the salon around the corner from my parent's bakery. I think I can get them to go," says Jamal confidently.

"What they look like," says Kenny concerned.

"I think they're both cute, but the one girl got an attitude problem I think," says Jamal recollecting the incident. "The one and only time I talked to her, she came off to me like she was Ms. Bitch, and I had to put her in her place."

"So why bring her?" Kenny asks.

"My parents and a mutual friend of ours have been tryin' to hook us up," says Jamal. "Home girl keeps tellin' me she's kool, but, I don't know. Every time I go to see her, I keep missing her."

"You think she's playin' games?" says Kenny.

"No," says Jamal, sure of himself. "Just a luck of the draw I guess. But at least this way, we can be around each other and she can see what I'm about, instead of stereotypin' me like she did last time."

"Well," says Kenny standing up. "I think you should invite them. If we got two already on board, I think we should go with it. I mean, it can't turn out that bad if you already know them."

"True," says Jamal thinking about it.

"Jamal, I'm about to go take this test," says Kenny, getting his things together. "Hit me up when you get an answer from those girls."

"Okay," says Jamal giving Kenny a handshake. "Will do. Oh, and good luck on that test."

"Thanks," says Kenny as he goes off to find an open computer.

*   *   *

"Hey Mom...," Jamal asked anxiously.

"Yeeesss," Beverly replied.

"Did you guys come to a consensus about letting me use the RV for my trip to Florida?" Jamal asked.

"Yes we did," says Beverly. "But there's one condition..."

"What's that?" says Jamal.

"You have to keep up everything on the RV by yourself. No help from us," Beverly answered.

"I can do that," says Jamal without a problem.

"Do you remember what to check to make sure everything's working?" says Beverly.

"Yeah, I remember," says Jamal. "Make sure the water pumps work, flush the dump tank frequently, check the generator to make sure it's able to run when you need it to, and check the engine. Check the engine fluids to make sure it's topped off and check the oil to see if I need to do an oil change **before** I leave. Am I missing anything?"

"Yes, you are," says Beverly. "Don't forget to check your outside lights. Front and back. Like the lights for your turn-signal, head-lights, and brake-lights."

"Ok Mom," says Jamal. "I got it... can I have the keys?"

Beverly stands up and pulls the keys out of her pocket. Then she slowly walks to Jamal, lifts his right hand up, and puts the keys in the center of his hand. He closes it. And as she inhales and gives him a big hug, she exhales, pulls back some and says, "I'm so proud of you, Jamal. Have a safe trip."

"Thank you Mom," says Jamal. "And I will."

Jamal walks out the front door and heads to the back of the shop where the garage and the recreational vehicle (RV) are.

*　　　*　　　*

While Jamal is working on the RV, he gets a visitor. It's Emily. "Hey Jamal," says Emily. "What are you doing?"

Jamal sticks his head up surprised, "Oh hey. I'm just inspecting this RV to make sure everything is up to par before I take it on the road in a couple days. And speaking of which, I was just about to call you at the salon to see if you and home girl wanted to go."

"That's funny," says Emily. "I was just about to ask you if you wanted to go to lunch with us or something. Maybe come hang out at the salon with us. Where're you going?"

"Remember that job I was tellin' Linda about the last time I saw her?" says Jamal.

"Yeah," says Emily.

"Well," says Jamal. "I got the job, and they're sending me to a conference in Orlando to give a presentation on kids and adults ability to learn through multiple intelligences."

45

"How long will we be gone?" asks Emily.

"We'll be gone for about a week," Jamal answers. "The conference is on Friday and Saturday of next week. So I figure we could leave this coming Saturday or Sunday."

"Hmm," says Emily thinking. "We should be able to go," says Emily. "I'm goin' to say yes now, but I'll talk to Linda about it and let you know later on today. Are you going to be here the rest of the day?"

"I'll be here until 2:30, 3:00," says Jamal.

"Okay. I'll call you by then," says Emily.

"Oh, and by the way," says Jamal. "I got a friend of mine coming with me too."

"Is it a guy?" says Emily concerned.

"Yeah," says Jamal. "He's kool, though. I go to school with him. And if you like me, then you'll like him."

"So you're making this a couple's trip," says Emily.

"I mean, if that's how things turn out, then yeah," says Jamal. "I'm not sayin' you should hook up with him. But if you like him, then go for it."

"Okay," says Emily. "That shouldn't be a problem."

"Okay, kool," says Jamal.

"I'll talk to you later," says Emily.

"Al'ight. I'll be here," says Jamal.

"Bye," says Emily.

Chapter 11

Jamal's friend walks into the bakery, wearing a book bag, and carrying a duffle bag. "Hi, is Jamal here?" Kenny asked Beverly, who's resting at the counter.

"You must be Jamal's friend who's going with him on his trip to Florida," says Beverly smiling.

"That's correct ma'am," Kenny responded.

"I'll go get him," says Beverly. "What's your name?"

"Kenny," Kenny answers.

"Pleasure meeting you Mr. Kenny," says Beverly responding.

"Likewise," Kenny replied.

"I am Mrs. Williams, Jamal's mom," says Beverly heading to the back.

"Oh, and Mr. Kenny," says Beverly stopping in mid stride and smiling. "Don't tear up my RV. Bring it back the same way you found it."

"Yes ma'am," says Kenny.

"I'll go get Jamal," says Beverly. "He may be a minute."

Beverly then walks to the back to let Jamal know his friend is here. She finds him talking with his father at the cake-decorating counter.

"… and that's how you know you've got em for good," says Charles, Jamal's father, standing at the counter, slouched over a bit. Gripping the air with his hands in front of him.

And Jamal is also standing there, actively listening.

"Jamal," says Beverly.

Jamal breaks his focus on his dad, and looks at his mom answering, "Yes Mom."

"Your friend, Kenny, is here with his things," says Beverly.

"Ok Mom. Here I come," says Jamal.

Beverly walks back up front to the counter.

"Dad," says Jamal, "I…"

"You know Jamal," says Jamal's dad, cutting Jamal off. "There comes a time, in a man's life, where he lays the foundation he can build the rest of his life on… and this is it."

Charles grabs Jamal, gives him a hug, and says, "I love you son." He pulls back and says, "Make the right choices while you're out there. And I'll see you when you get back."

"I will Dad," says Jamal.

Jamal then leaves the back of the bakery and walks up front, along the counter and says, "Yo, what's good?" giving Kenny a handshake once he walked around the counter.

"Not much," says Kenny. "Ready to hit this road."

"Okay bet," says Jamal. "Let's roll out. Bye Mom."

Jamal and Kenny leave the bakery and walk to the RV, which is parked right in front of the bakery. Jamal leads

Kenny to the side door of the RV. He unlocks it and goes inside. Kenny follows right behind him.

Once inside, Jamal shows Kenny where he can put his things and his options on where he can sleep when he gets tired. Shortly after that, Jamal makes his way to the driver's seat. Once he sits in the seat, he puts the key in the ignition and starts the RV. Jamal then calls the salon to let them know he's on his way. Then, Jamal puts the gear in drive, checks his surroundings for traffic, then he pulls off.

Jamal pulls up in front of the salon, and puts the RV in park with the hazard lights on. The girls (Linda and Emily) see the RV parked in front of their salon, and they start getting their things together.

Linda says, "Girl, I can't believe I let you talk me into this."

"It's going to be fun. Just loosen up a little," says Emily.

"Oh, and Shelly, don't forget to make the deposit at the bank, after you've closed the salon," says Linda. "Remember, the deposit is 120 minus the total cash you have on hand."

"Okay, I got it," Shelly responds. "And I'll send you a copy of the deposits when I close up."

"Great. I'll see you when I get back," says Linda.

"Bye, you guys. Have fun," says Shelly.

The girls then make their way out of the salon and to the RV.

"Here they come," says Kenny looking out of the passenger seat window. "Not bad. The girl in the back is for you?"

"Uuhhh," says Jamal, struggling to look out of a window without being seen. "Does she have long hair?"

"Yeah. She doesn't look happy," says Kenny.

"Yeah that's her," says Jamal. "She probably doesn't want to go… or she's getting cold feet." Jamal looks out the window a little more and says, making himself laugh, "Unless she's got resting-bitch-face-syndrome or something."

The handle on the side door starts to jiggle for a moment. Then the door slowly opens.

"Hi guys," says Emily stepping inside the RV, sounding excited. "How are you?"

Forgetting his manners, Jamal jumps up to help the girls into the RV and answers, "I'm doing fine, Emily, this is Kenny. Kenny, this is Emily."

"Hi, how are you," says Emily extending her hand to shake Kenny's hand.

"I'm fine, and yourself," says Kenny meeting her hand with his, shaking it briefly.

"I'm good," says Emily. "And Jamal, you met Linda before."

"Yeah. Uuhh… hi," says Jamal thinking about their last conversation. And trying to not let things get awkward between them, he sticks his hand out to shake her hand. She meets his hand with hers, but only gives him half her hand.

"And Linda, this is Kenny, one of Jamal's friends," says Emily.

"Hi," says Linda bringing her things with her as she sits at the table.

"Okay, let me give you a quick tour of the place," says Jamal. "So you can know where to put your things. Where we're at right now is the common area or living room, slash kitchen. And in front of that, is pretty obvious, is the cab or cabin. That's where I'll be. Driving this thing all the way to Florida and makin' a few stops along the way. Okay, you can follow me or stay where you are; but,

50

behind the kitchen is the bathroom toilet on one side, and a shower on the other side. Behind the toilet, is a water heater and a closet where you can put your things. You can leave them there, or put your things in some of the cabinets that are pretty much placed throughout this RV. Behind the shower is a regular bathroom sink and medicine cabinet. And then when you go past there, is where I'll be sleeping. In the bedroom. Um, you can leave your stuff in there, too, for the time being if you want."

"Question," says Emily.

"Yes," Jamal responds.

"Where are we going to be sleeping, if you have the only bed in here," says Emily.

"Glad you asked," says Jamal. "The couch in the common area, is a futon. You have the floor. You can sleep in the booth, in the common area. The bed in the bedroom is a full size or queen. I can stomach sleeping with another person as long as you don't snore. And then, you have the passenger seat in the cab. Anymore questions about sleeping arrangements or anything in general."

"I think that's about it," says Emily looking at Linda and Kenny.

"Great," says Jamal feeling like everyone is on the same page. "I'm about to go jump in the cab and get this trip started. You guys can chill back here and get to know each other or something."

Jamal goes to the cab and jumps in the driver's seat. Emily gives Linda a nudge, to go with Jamal and sit in the passenger seat to keep him company. Linda fights with Emily briefly, then walks to the cab's passenger seat.

"You mind if I sit?" Linda asks.

"Nah. Go ahead," Jamal responds. Putting his seat belt on. "There's only one rule I have if you're going to ride with me in any vehicle."

"What's that," says Linda sitting in the passenger seat.

"You have to wear that seat belt," says Jamal checking his blind spots and the traffic.

Linda mouths, "you have to wear a seat belt" shaking her head, imitating Jamal. Borderline making fun of him while she is putting the seatbelt on.

Jamal looks at Linda, and she has a surprised look on her face because she's not sure if he heard her or not.

"You know there's an elephant in the room," says Jamal.

"You mean RV," says Linda correcting him.

"Why not," Jamal responds. Then he puts his head down, and wipes his hands, slowly over his face; trying to keep himself together. Then he thinks about what he is going to say next.

Linda sees Jamal going through something over there in the driver's seat and she thinks she caused it. So, out of fear that he would ask her to leave the cabin, she musters up enough courage to say something. So she opens her mouth to say something, and at the same time, Jamal says, "I came by the salon…" And Linda says, "I'm sorry about…" Then they both stopped.

Jamal then says, holding his hand out briefly, "Lady's first."

"Okay," says Linda preparing herself to admit fault. "I'm sorry about how I acted the other day. You must think I'm an asshole or something."

"I'd be lying if I said the thought didn't cross my mind," says Jamal. "But I had a different adjective in mind when it went down. And don't worry about it. It's all good. I accept your apology."

"What were you about to say?" Linda asks.

"Oh," says Jamal. "I came by the salon a couple of times to try and smooth things over, but I kept missing you for some reason."

"Yeah, it's funny you say that, 'cause I came by the bakery looking for you, hoping to apologize for my behavior," says Linda opening up some and feeling relieved. "I even placed an order to try to get you to come to the salon, but I had to run to the bank. I thought I'd be back in time to catch you, but it didn't work out that way."

"Yeah, well here's a little FYI," says Jamal with a smile on his face. "I had already forgiven you. And if we met up, I was going to suggest that we start over or something, because we didn't get off to a good start."

"That's, actually a good idea," says Linda, invested. "Can we start over?"

"Sure," says Jamal excited. "Hi! My name is Jamal. I need a job, **and**, can I get your number so I can 'talk' to you."

"Shut, up," says Linda hitting Jamal in the arm laughing.

Jamal, also laughing, says, "What? I just want to know if you're hiring and got a boyfriend."

Linda laughs hysterically.

"I'm sayin'," says Jamal. "I'm tryin' to put in an application for both jobs."

Linda laughs still.

"Can you hook a brotha up," says Jamal laughin' a bit.

"Oh my gosh, you are too funny," says Linda holding her stomach catching her breath. "You got my stomach hurting." Linda starts stretching her stomach muscles with one hand in the air leaning to one side. And then she puts her other hand in the air and leans to the other side. She then puts her hands behind her back and leans back some. Linda says, "Oh my God. I feel like I just did a thousand sit-ups."

"So we good now?" Jamal asks.

"Yeah... we're good," says Linda still recovering.

"So I can pull off now?" Jamal asks.

"Yes. Let's," says Linda.

Jamal shifts the gear to "drive," checks the road for traffic, sets the RV in motion, and the road trip officially begins.

Chapter 12

"Okay. Now that that's out of the way, what do you have planned for this week-long trip to Florida," Linda asks. Trying to be serious for a moment. Still recovering from laughing so hard.

"Okay," says Jamal. "Here's what's going on. I just got this new job at Virtex as a programmer. And I have to basically do a survey of a sample size population and record the data I collect. It's supposed to help determine, in kids and adults, the best way they are able to learn. And, highlight what the best method of educating them is."

"So what do you guys do with this information," Linda asks.

"I guess they're going to sell the software and information to school districts across the country," says Jamal unsure of himself. "I mean if you think about it, logically, that would be the next step. But I don't know. I didn't really ask too much about that 'cause I was still trying to wrap my head around the fact that they wanted to send me to Florida and represent the company."

"And that's another thing. You're new to the job and they're already sending you on a company trip," Linda says in disbelief.

"Yeah," says Jamal confidently. "The reason for that, my manager said, is because I'm one of a very few people that checked "willing to travel" on my application. Then, when I was getting interviewed, he asked me again about traveling and I told him how much I like it. And to be an ambassador for a company is an honor for me. Because I have a business acumen that's pretty good, and representing a company is not something I take for granted. It means a lot to me."

"So how do you plan on getting these surveys done?" Linda asks.

"Well, my plan is to hit every mall and shopping center, on the way down there," says Jamal. "Or, wherever there's a large gathering of people. But for right now, those are the only places I can think of."

"Do you have a certain number of people in mind you're tryin' to survey or just a handful of malls and shopping centers," Linda asks.

"I was told, from my boss, to 'survey at least five hundred people'," says Jamal. "And it makes sense, too. 'Cause if you think about it, in order for the data collected to be consistent and cover all areas of learning, about 500 or more, from both children and adults, should be enough to cover it."

"And you plan on doing that all by yourself?" Linda asks.

"Well, that's where you guys come in," says Jamal. "They gave me everything I need to conduct these surveys. I've got a few tables, table covers, iPads, printers and some other promotional tools and equipment. And to really make us look legit, I got a couple of polo shirts to help us look like we work for a company... or so to speak."

"So you just knew we would help you," says Linda.

"No, I didn't," says Jamal. "Kenny is already in, and I figure it'll be something fun for all of us to do since it's not labor intensive. But it's completely up to you if you want to get involved or not."

"What do I have to do?" asks Linda, going along with it.

"Okay, it's real simple," says Jamal. "All you have to do is start a session on the iPad, I'll show you how to do that, give it to the kid or adult to answer the questions. When they're done, they'll give you back the iPad and you give them the results that print out of the printer and you're done."

Linda looks behind her to check on Emily and sees that she's at the table with Kenny talking. She then turns back around and looks at Jamal. This time, she's analyzing his face. Looking at every inch of it. Then she asks him, "Have I met you before?"

Jamal, focused on the road at this point, gives her a glance and says, "I'd remember you if we did. What makes you say that?"

"Nothing," says Linda. "Just wondering. I feel like I've seen you before."

"I'm sure if we did, our encounter at the salon would have been very different," says Jamal.

Linda doesn't say anything. She pulls her phone out of her pants pocket and checks the time. It's just past noon.

Chapter 13

Everything is quiet. All you hear is the air coming in from the open windows in the cab. Linda, who's looking out of the window, turns back around to see what Emily's doing, and she's not at the table. But Kenny is. And from the looks of it, he's reading a book. But she can't tell too much because his back is towards her.

To break the silence, Linda says to Jamal, "Your last name is Williams, right? Like your mom and dad?"

"Yeah," says Jamal glancing over at Linda. "Jamal Williams, that's me. What about you, what's your full name?"

"Mine is Linda Harper," says Linda. "And my middle name is Justice."

"Justice," says Jamal surprised some. "You mean like 'Justice League' Justice?"

"Batman and Superman," says Linda.

"Yeah," says Jamal trying to keep his eyes on the road.

"That's it," says Linda watching the road.

A few moments later, Linda says to Jamal, "Hey Jamal, what are we going to do for food on this trip? Does the fridge have anything in it?"

"I bought some lunch meat, peanut butter and jelly, and two loaves of bread" says Jamal. "I figure we could eat a couple of sandwiches. Go out to eat here and there, maybe. And if you don't like that, I guess we could go to the supermarket."

Something in the air catches Jamal's attention. Jamal starts sniffing the air and says, "You smell that?"

"Yeah I do actually," says Linda sitting up in her seat. And she starts sniffing the air, too. "It smells really good."

"You could go to the supermarket," says Jamal trying to finish his thought. He then sees a bunch of cars parked off to the right and says, "Or you could go to a barbeque... what you think?"

"We don't know that for sure," says Linda. "Plus, that food ain't for us anyway."

"You want to bet," says Jamal turning into the park entrance. "Let's see if they're barbequing first, then we'll see if we can grab something to eat."

Looking for a place to park in the parking lot, Jamal sees a banner saying "Johnson Family Reunion." Jamal then says, "Hey Linda... they're barbequing."

"And we're not family," says Linda immediately.

"Yes we are," says Jamal finding a parking spot. "We just got to play the part."

Jamal turns the engine off.

Jamal then looks at Linda and says, "You look the part to me."

"Yeah, well I'm Indian," Linda says defensively.

Jamal responds, "Yeah, me too... on my father's side. Let me guess... Cherokee?"

Linda rolls her eyes and Jamal unbuckles his seatbelt and climbs out of the cab into the common area.

"Hey Kenny," says Jamal. "There's a barbeque going on in the park and we're about to see if we can get some food. You want to go?"

"I was wondering what that smell was," says Kenny, putting his book down on the table.

"Barbeque? What y'all say about a barbeque?" says Emily coming from the bedroom.

Linda unbuckles her seatbelt, gets up from the passenger seat, and walks to the table saying, "Jamal wants to see if we can get some free barbeque."

"And what's wrong with that?" says Emily.

"It's at a family reunion and we're not family," Linda says.

"Linda, we're all family when it comes to a barbeque," says Emily.

"Look," says Jamal. "All we have to do is find out if they ate yet. And if they did, we'll just get in line."

"Yeah, well, what if they didn't. Then what?" Linda says.

"We'll just fit in until it's time to eat," says Jamal confidently. "We can find somebody that's kool and just kick it with them or something."

"I'm game," says Kenny moving to the edge of the booth.

"Me too," says Emily standing there.

Jamal then looks at Linda and she sighs and says holding her hand out, "Lead the way."

Jamal, Linda, Emily, and Kenny walk out of the RV and Jamal locks the door behind him.

"Remember," says Jamal looking at the group. "All we have to do is act the part." He then looks at Kenny and Emily and says, "And look like we're together."

Jamal then starts to walk off and Linda follows right behind him, along with Emily and Kenny. They casually walk across the parking lot and on to the grass. Once they're there, Jamal sees the picnic tables with people sitting there and it's hard to tell whether or not they ate because the plates are scattered about. And it looks like some have food on them, and some don't. Jamal locates the barbeque grill and there's a big man standing in front of it cooking the food, moving it around, and placing it into aluminum pans that are sitting off to the side. And at one of the picnic tables close to him, is a group of older women with gray hair. And with confidence, Jamal makes his way to that table with his friends following behind him. Jamal approaches the table and says smiling, "Hey Grandmom, how are you doing?"

"I'm fine, baby," says Grandmom. "What can I do you for?"

Jamal answers comfortably, "I know we showed up a little late, but I was wondering if everybody ate already, or are we still waiting."

While Jamal is talking to Grandmom and everyone at the table, he is approached by a woman.

"Well there she is right there," says Grandmom.

Jamal turns around and is greeted with the question, "Can I help you with something?"

"Jamal, this is Silvia," says Grandmom. "Silvia this is Jamal and his friends. They were just about to get something to eat."

"Oh really," says Silvia very sternly crossing her arms. "Which side of the family you on, 'cause you don't look like family to me."

Jamal looks at Linda trying to come up with an answer. Linda looks at Emily and back at Jamal. Then Jamal looks back at Silvia defeated. Linda then speaks up and says,

61

cutting in the conversation, "We're from Virtex and we were wondering if you and your entire family would like to take a survey that measures your kids' and adults' ability to learn. And find what the best method of learning for them is."

"You don't look like you're from any company," says Silvia looking at their clothes.

Jamal says jumping in, "All of our tools and equipment used to take the survey are back at my RV. Let us set everything up, and you can come try us out."

Unmoved Silvia looks towards the parking lot for an RV, then looks back at them. After a moment, she says, "How long does this survey take?"

"Five to ten minutes max," says Jamal relieved.

"Okay," says Silvia interested. "Let's see this survey."

"Okay, great," says Jamal. "Give us ten minutes to set up, then meet us over there at the RV."

Jamal looks at his friends and says, "Let's go set up."

Jamal and his friends start walking back to the RV.

"Thanks for getting my back, back there," says Jamal.

"You're welcome, but we don't know what we're doing," says Linda.

"Nah, it's all good," says Jamal. "Remember what I said about the survey? All you got to do is open the app and start a session and that's it. They put in whatever information is needed after that."

Jamal and his friends get back to the RV. Jamal unlocks the door to the RV and then goes to the storage area below the RV and starts unlocking the doors that have the equipment in it. And before he forgets, Jamal pulls out the awning on the side of the RV. Next, Jamal gets the box with the company polos and gives it to Linda and Emily and they both go inside to change.

"Hey Kenny," says Jamal with his hand on the table ready to pull it out. "Give me a hand with this table."

"Yeah, no problem," says Kenny.

Jamal and Kenny pull the table out from the storage area under the RV and set it up. Next Jamal gets the box that has the iPads and computer in it and sets it on the table. Then he gets the printer, monitor, banners, and the table cloth with the company name on it from the storage and sets it on the table. Then Jamal pulls out a smaller table and sets it up next to the big table on the side. Jamal moves everything from the big table to the smaller table so he can cover the table with the table cloth. Kenny moves to set up the banners. Jamal then says, "When you get done setting those up, put one on one side of this table and the other on the other side. But not too close. Set them farther out."

"Okay, I got you," says Kenny.

Just as he says that, Linda and Emily come out of the RV dressed with the company shirt on. Jamal turns the computer on and sets out the iPads; also turning them on. Once the computer's on, he logs on and connects it to the monitor. Then he starts the video that promotes the company and talks about the survey. Kenny then goes inside to change his shirt. Once Jamal plugs in the printer and turns it on, he connects all the devices to the printer, then goes inside to change. When Jamal is inside changing his shirt, Silvia, her husband, and kids walk up to the table and start looking and reading everything. Jamal and Kenny then come out of the RV, dressed, with the company shirts on.

"So, the surveys are on this iPad I take it..." says Silvia.

"Jamal," says Jamal finishing her sentence. "This is Linda, Kenny, and Emily. But yes, you take the survey here on one of these iPads and your results print out over here on the printer, along with some recommendations."

"Okay," says Silvia. "This is my husband Joe. And these are our kids Evan and Tommy."

"Babe," says Silvia to her husband. "You and the kids take the survey first, then go back and tell everyone else, especially the kids, to come over here and take the survey."

"Ok kids, you heard your mother," says Joe. "Now, what do we do here," says Joe, picking up an iPad.

"All you have to do is enter your information here," says Jamal looking at the iPad screen, and pointing. "And when you're done with that, it'll start asking you questions. And after that, you're done. The results will print out at the printer."

"Oh and I forgot to put these out," says Jamal going inside the box and pulling out a stack of marketing materials about the company, the program, and how the survey measures your ability to learn. He sets a small stack behind the iPad on the left and he puts another small stack on the right.

Silvia takes a sheet and starts reading it. And just as she's about done reading it, her husband and her kids finish almost simultaneously. Her husband smiles, impressed by the survey, putting the iPad back on the table and says, "I do like learning hands on and through video. Kids, what you get?"

"We both got reading," says Evan.

Linda immediately says going towards the printer, "Don't forget your printout." And she takes the printed paper and hands them to the kids and the husband.

"Kids," says Silvia, "Let me see your results."

The kids give her their results and she reads it immediately. Almost studying it.

"Come on kids," says Joe walking away from the setup. "Let's go get some of your cousins to come over here."

Silvia folds her children's and husbands results and puts it in her back pocket. Then she picks up an iPad and starts filling out the required information. Within a few minutes she's finished and family members start arriving and asking questions.

Even though Linda, Emily, and Kenny weren't as well versed with the information as Jamal was, a lot of the questions were repeated. And Jamal jumped in, to help, whenever it was necessary.

At the end of it all, Jamal, Linda, Emily, and Kenny were beat. They were dead tired as unanticipated for just giving a survey.

"Well, I think everything went okay," said Jamal looking at everyone. "What did you think, Linda, of how things turned out?"

"I think things turned out fine," said Linda standing up and brushing herself off. "I just need to read some more information about multiple intelligences and see how this survey is able to measure everyone's ability to learn."

Linda then grabbed one of the marketing papers left on the table and says, reading it, "I'm not saying I need to understand the entire mechanics of it all, but, I need to learn enough to feel comfortable and confident with my answers."

"I hear ya," says Kenny sitting on the gravel with a wash rag over his face.

In the middle of them resting under the awning of the RV and talking amongst themselves, someone had approached their setup. It was Silvia.

"How did things go for you all today," says Silvia.

"It went well, all things considered," says Jamal. "I just got to go over the information gathered for my report."

"That's good to hear," says Silvia. "Uh, listen... if you guys aren't in a hurry, we wouldn't mind if you guys came to eat with us. You've helped some of us out quite a bit, and there's plenty of food for everyone."

"Oh, we thought you already ate," says Linda looking at Jamal.

"Some of us did, here and there, but the majority of us are lining up now," says Silvia.

"Say no more, we're coming right behind you," says Jamal. "We just have to pack everything away first."

"Okay," says Silvia. "We'll see you when you get over there." Silvia then walks off, heading back towards the park.

"I told you we could get some free barbeque," says Jamal smiling, putting the iPads in a box.

"Well, it's not like it was free," says Linda. "We did have to work for it."

"Not really," says Jamal clearing the tables. "We was going to do the surveys anyway."

"Yeah right boy," says Linda moving out of the way. "Doin' those surveys was the last thing on your mind."

"Even so, it would have came to me eventually," says Jamal tipping the table over. "Oh, and don't forget to take the shirts off so you don't get any barbeque stains on it."

"Good idea," says Linda following behind Emily, going inside the RV.

"So, what do you think," says Emily excited with a smile on her face, making her way to the bedroom. "He's kool, right?"

"I guess so," says Linda taking her shirt off. "I thought he was goin' to be very controlling with his setup and how he wanted things to go. But I guess I was wrong." Linda puts her original shirt back on and starts fixing her hair.

Emily, doing the same says, "So, you goin' to give him a shot?"

"I don't know just yet," says Linda leaning against the closet, hiding the truth; waiting for Emily to finish getting ready. "It depends on how he treats me while we're on this trip."

"Mmm-hmm. Well do you at least think he's cute?" says Emily finishing her hair.

"I think he's cute," says Linda. Again, hiding the truth; walking to the front of the RV with Emily close behind her. "Enough about me, what do you think about Kenny?"

"I think he's kool," says Emily hiding the truth like Linda did. "But we'll probably end up just being friends or something."

"Okay, girl," says Linda opening the side door. "You ain't got to lie to me."

They then leave out the side door on the RV.

As the girls come out of the RV, Jamal and Kenny slide the table back under the RV in the storage compartment. And they put the boxes back under there as well. Once Jamal locks up the storage compartments, he retracts the awning and sets it back against the RV. Then Jamal and Kenny go inside the RV, as they did before, to change their shirts.

"So bro, what do you think about Linda," says Kenny grabbing his shirt from off the couch and changing into it.

"Well, when she first came in, we had to clear the air, because, I wasn't about to be stuck with someone who is full of them self and is a know-it-all," says Jamal taking his shirt off and grabbing his original shirt, from the seat in the booth, and putting it on. "People like that you can't tell them anything. But she's proven herself to be down to earth and easy goin'. I can tell at the end of it all, she just wants to have a good time. What about you? What do you think about Emily?"

"I'm not sure yet if I can put her on my team or not," says Kenny. "She's a little hard to read. She's friendly, I'll give her that. But anything more than that, I don't know."

"She could be playing hard to get," says Jamal leaning against the table.

"And I thought about that too," says Kenny sitting on the arm of the couch. "Hopefully I'll find out sooner than later."

"Yeah, hopefully," says Jamal agreeing with him. "You ready to go eat?"

"Yeah. Let's get out of here," says Kenny walking to the side door and opening it.

Jamal and Kenny make their way out of the RV. Jamal locks the door behind him and they head over to the park.

Chapter 14

Once they're at the park, they get in line to get some food. And while they are in line, Linda overhears someone in line ahead of her, talking about having to rent the pavilion from Parks and Recreation in order to have the family reunion there. Parks and Recreation also puts the events on their online calendar in order to let people know what's going on at their parks. She looks at Jamal, who is standing right behind her, to see if he hears what she just heard. And he's not paying any attention. Linda gets an idea and can't wait to tell Jamal. But she keeps it to herself until she's able to check things out for herself.

Once Linda gets her food, she waits for Jamal to finish loading up his plate. She then follows him to a wooden picnic table and sits next to him. Kenny and Emily soon follows behind them and follows suit. Emily sits next to Kenny.

Jamal bows his head, opens his hands in front of him and starts to pray over his food quietly. Linda places her hand in his as he's praying and he stops for a moment. He opens his eyes, and look towards his hand. Then he looks at Linda and she has her head bowed the same way Jamal does. Jamal returns his head to the bowed position and continues to pray. This time, a little louder so Linda can hear him and follow along.

After they get done praying over their food, they start eating that food like they haven't eaten all day. When they've finished, Linda sees Jamal get up and fill his plate again. This time he wraps foil around it and walks back to the wooden picnic table. Linda looks at him in disbelief. And Jamal looks back at her and says laughing, "What? As good as this food was, you ain't think about makin' yourself a plate?"

Linda shakes her head laughing, gets up from the table and says, "You do have a point." Then she walks off to the table with the food on it.

When Linda gets back to the wooden picnic table, Jamal is on the phone. So she takes this opportunity to research the information she heard earlier about Parks and Recreation posting events on their calendar online. And while she's at it, she remembered that Yahoo posts events locally on their website too. And she checked there also.

Shortly after Jamal gets off the phone, Linda finished doing her "research." Jamal then asks Kenny and Emily, "Are y'all ready to go? We got a lot of ground to cover."

"Yeah," said Kenny. "We was just about to ask you the same thing."

"Okay," says Jamal getting up from the table. "Let me go tell that lady we're leaving, and thanks for the food. Meet me back at the RV."

"Okay, bet," says Kenny, leaving the wooden picnic table with Emily.

Jamal turns to start walking and Linda stands in front of him. She looks into his eyes, and says, "Is it okay if I come with you?"

Trying not to read too much into her question, Jamal replies, "Sure. Come on." And they start looking for Silvia, who happened to be close by.

Silvia approaches Jamal and Linda head on saying, "How'd you guys enjoy your meal."

"The food was great," says Jamal. "It was so good, I made a second plate to take with me." Jamal lifts up his plate some, showing her.

"We all did," says Linda showing her plate as well with a pleasant look on her face.

"We were looking for you to let you know we was leaving, and we wanted to say thank you for participating in the survey," says Jamal. "And thank you for the food."

"You guys are welcome," says Silvia. "And thank you for the survey. I looked up some of that information on the internet. And I think I found a way to help my kids learn the information, that they are taught in school, better. And any time we have a cookout, you're more than welcome."

Silvia walks in and gives Jamal a hug. Then she gives Linda a hug.

Silvia then says, "Have a safe trip."

"Thanks," says Jamal. "We will... I'll see you later."

Silvia waves her hand, walking off and says, "Bye."

"Bye," says Linda.

Linda and Jamal both walk off towards the RV.

*   *   *

Jamal approaches the RV and Emily and Kenny are standing by the side door waiting for Jamal. Jamal stops and looks at the situation presented to him. And he says, "Damn, I guess I could've given you the keys so you didn't have to wait outside. My bad."

"Nah, you good," says Kenny. "We would have been out here anyway... well, I know I would have."

Jamal pulls his keys out from his pocket, unlocks and opens the side door on the RV. Everyone goes inside and Jamal is the last one in. While inside, everyone is getting settled and Jamal puts his plate in the refrigerator. Then he makes his way to the cab and gets in the driver's seat. Jamal puts the key in the ignition, pulls out his phone, and starts searching the maps application for the nearest mall and shopping center.

While Jamal is on his phone, searching for the next place to go, Linda comes to the cab and sits in the passenger seat and says, "Hey, before you take off, there's something I want to show you."

Interested, Jamal responds, "What's that?"

"I found a list of more barbeques and outside events taking place over the next couple of days from here, all the way down to Florida," says Linda. "The malls and shopping centers doesn't have to be the only place we go to do the surveys."

"Let me see that," says Jamal holding out his hand. Linda gives him her phone. "How'd you find out about this," says Jamal looking through the online calendar dates.

"I overheard someone at the barbeque say something about Parks and Recreation publishing a calendar of events, happening at the parks," says Linda. "I also remembered that Yahoo does the same thing. But instead of parks, they do it with local events."

"That's a good idea," says Jamal, handing Linda back her phone.

"And if we go to the events happening at the parks, we could get free food like we did today," says Linda looking at Jamal.

"Okay," says Jamal. "Let's do both, because I'm goin' to have to restock on ink and paper for the printer."

Linda agrees.

Then Jamal says, "We can go to the park events around noon time. And when we get done with that, we can go to the mall or the shopping center."

Chapter 15

Later on that evening, thinking about the way things were going with the survey, it dawned on Jamal that he didn't even take the survey. Nor did anybody else who was on this trip with him. So how could they possibly relate to the people who took it. So Jamal took it upon himself to go in the storage and get an iPad and the printer and take the survey himself; along with everybody else. Jamal set up the printer and turned on the iPad in the booth. While Jamal was taking the survey, he noticed that information being taken by the program was universal for both kids and adults. While the age range was being recorded, the test itself remained the same. Jamal then calls for Linda, "Hey Linda. Can you come here for a second?"

Linda walks to the common area where Jamal is and answers him. "You called me Jamal," says Linda.

"Yeah," says Jamal. "Hey, did you get a chance to take the survey?"

"No," says Linda. "I didn't know we had to."

"You don't," says Jamal. "But I think you should, to help better relate to the people we're giving the survey too. I mean, I think we all should."

"So is that what you want me to do," says Linda sitting across from Jamal.

"Yes, it is," says Jamal, handing her the iPad.

"And while you're doing that…," says Jamal. He gets up and goes outside to the storage looking for the laptop.

After a few moments, Jamal comes back inside the RV, with a laptop in his hands, and sits back at his seat in the booth, and opens the computer.

"What's that for," Linda asks while still taking the survey.

"I'm looking at the reports generated from taking the survey," says Jamal typing and clicking away at the computer. "Here it is," says Jamal to himself.

"You want me to print it," Linda asks.

"Yes," Jamal answers. "… damn."

"What's wrong," says Linda getting up from her seat and sitting next to Jamal.

"Nothin' too serious… some of the answers from the questions aren't posting to the report for some reason," says Jamal intrigued.

Linda starts to analyze his face again. But this time she's looking at his entire head. She notices, this time, his broad shoulders. Next, she pulls her legs in and sits on them. Linda then takes a peak at the upper part of his back. The part that the shirt allows her to see, and she wants more. It's at this moment she realizes how attractive he is to her. And almost without thought, she very carefully, touches the back of Jamal's neck where his hairline is, with her finger tips, and slowly drags them down the center of his neck, where his vertebrae is; to slightly past the collar.

Jamal's concentration is broken for a moment and then he turns his head to her. And Linda, who falls in love with him, pulls him in with the hand that's still on his neck, leans her head to the side, closes her eyes, and begins to kiss Jamal on his lips... and he goes for it. Linda wraps her other arm around him and sucks on his bottom lip.

"I knew it," says Emily out loud, standing in front of the refrigerator.

Linda and Jamal break their connection.

"The second I heard it get quiet from all that talking, I knew something was up, says Emily."

"And I sat here and watched the whole thing," says Kenny trying to gain some brownie points with Emily, sitting on the couch. "They must have forgot I was sitting here."

"Nobody forgot about you or you," says Jamal getting himself together. "As a matter of fact, since I got both of y'all's attention, I need you to take the survey." Jamal hands the iPad to Emily.

And she responds, "Oh no. You ain't goin' to try and shut me up. We need to talk about this."

"No we don't," says Linda getting up from the booth, walking to the refrigerator, and grabbing a canned iced tea out of the refrigerator. And then sitting back in the booth.

"Fine," says Jamal. "Kenny. Here you go." Jamal hands the iPad to Kenny.

"I'd be thirsty too, if I had someone suckin' the life out of me the same way you two were goin' at it," says Emily.

"It was just a kiss," says Jamal.

"No it wasn't," says Emily. "If I hadn't of walked in here when I did, y'all would be in here makin' babies." Emily starts shaking her head.

"Hey Emily," says Jamal. "When Kenny gives you the iPad, don't take the survey yet. I'm about to make some changes to it."

"There's goin' to be some changes made alright," says Emily walking to the back. "Come on girl, so we can give Jamal his space. So he can finish programming whatever."

"I'll be back," says Linda. Slowly getting up, stickin' her butt out some. She looks behind herself to see if Jamal's watching, and he is. Then she disappears to the back.

Once Linda gets to the bedroom in the back, she drops herself on the bed next to Emily. Emily has a stern look on her face for a minute. Then she lights up and says, "Okay, girl. Tell me what happened."

Chapter 16

The next day, first thing in the morning, Jamal got clearance from Robert to change the survey. Once he made the necessary changes to the survey and tested it, he continued on his way to the next destination. To keep up with the time, Jamal and his "team" of people only attended two events a day. And an occasional stop to an office store to refill on supplies. On their way through the states to Orlando Florida, Jamal has come across other barbeques. But, the first of a few, Jamal wants to go to a wedding reception, and a Bar Mitzvah.

Jamal pulls into the parking lot, and he sees what could be the groom and the groomsman of the wedding, taking a smoke break. This couldn't be a better opportunity for Jamal to capitalize on getting a survey done for a couple that either has kids or are planning on having kids in the near future. Jamal parks the RV in the parking lot, towards the back, so it can give him space to setup.

"I can't believe we're going to crash a wedding," says Linda with her face in her hands.

Jamal then responds, "We're not going to crash their wedding. We're simply goin' to find out if they're interested in taking the survey. The same as any other time. I could see if we were selling something. Then that would be a different story."

"Okay," says Linda. "You want one of us to come with you?"

"No. I got this one," says Jamal confidently. He then unbuckles his seat belt and grabs a couple of the marketing papers and heads out the side door.

"I hope they don't kick him out," says Linda, looking out of the passenger window. Feeling a little nervous for Jamal, as he walks through the parking lot.

"They shouldn't," says Kenny looking out of the same window, sitting in the driver's seat. "I mean, like he said, it's not like he's asking for money. And, he's got the company polo on with a couple of those information sheets. So they should be able to see he's legit."

As Jamal approaches the group, he clears his throat, and says, speaking to everyone, "Excuse me, fellas. My name is Jamal Williams and I work for Virtex. I was wondering if I could interest you guys in taking a survey that measures your ability to learn."

"How much does it cost," says one of the groomsman.

"Nothing," says Jamal with a smile on his. "Just, literally, five minutes of your time. Here's some information on what they survey covers." Jamal hands the marketing paper to some of the groomsman. "Which one of you guys is getting married. I'd like to say congratulations."

"He's on his way out here," says the other groomsman.

"Now I understand this is a wedding reception, and you guys are probably on a smoke break, but I guarantee you this is worth your time," says Jamal.

"I wonder what he's saying to them," says Linda still looking out of the window.

"I don't know, but someone else just came outside," says Kenny.

"I see him," Linda responds. "And now he's talking to him."

"Let me see what all the fuss is about," says Emily looking around Linda to see out of the passenger window.

About a minute goes by and Linda says, "Okay, he's on his way back."

Everyone scrambles around in the RV to try and look naturally nonchalant. Then Jamal opens the side door and walks inside.

Linda says from the booth, "What did they say?"

Jamal looks at her, surprised at what he's about to say, and says, "They want to see what we got."

"Oh my God," says Linda. "That's good right?"

"Yeah," says Jamal smiling. "He even said his wife will be interested. So he's going to bring her and the bridesmaids, along with the groomsmen, because a couple of them have kids. But who knows. A few of the guests might come out too, if the word gets around."

"Wow, that's great Jamal," says Linda excited. "So what do we do now."

Jamal looks at Linda and says, "We set everything up."

*   *   *

With the concept of this survey being so well-liked, the next day, Jamal was able to gain acceptance to a Bar Mitzvah at the last minute. There, most of the adults liked it so much, they were ready to purchase the program on-site. And because the demand was so high, the adults demanded, Jamal talk to his boss about releasing the software ahead of time to them. Jamal's boss, Robert, ended up giving them exclusive access to a pre-sale, through their website, to purchase the program ahead of time; the second it becomes ready to go to market.

Chapter 17

Jamal has been on the road driving for about ten hours and the scenery looks like he's been driving through the wilderness with no civilization in site. Every so often he'll pass by a small town and shopping centers with a Target and Home Depot stores attached to them. And instead of there being a regular size gas station, he would come across super gas stations with a store or a fast food chain on one side; and directly next to it, with no separating door or wall, would be the actual gas station store. Knowing, from the signs on the road, that they just crossed into Florida, Jamal gives his Aunt Glenda a call to see if he can stop by for a visit. Halfway through the phone call, Jamal tries to keep the conversation short. And his Aunt understands.

"Are you sure, Aunt Glenda," says Jamal trying to focus more on the road, than the actual phone call, while he's driving. "I'm not trying to intrude or anything."

"...Okay," says Jamal.

"...For a couple days," says Jamal. "I'm going to a conference in Orlando."

"...Yeah," says Jamal answering. "I've got the RV with me and a couple of friends."

"...Can you text me the address," Jamal asks.

"Okay," says Jamal. "See you when I get there."

"Bye," says Jamal ending his call.

"Hey guys," says Jamal. "We just crossed into Florida. You mind if we swing by Kissimmee so I can visit my Aunt."

Everyone comes to the cab and stands right behind Jamal, looking out of the windshield. Linda makes her way into the passenger seat.

"Do you think we'll have time," Emily asks.

"We should," Jamal says. "It's only Wednesday. The conference starts on Friday. So I figure we can be out sometime Thursday night or something."

"Does your Aunt have free barbeque," Kenny asks.

"No," says Jamal laughing. "But if you want something to eat, I'm sure she won't have a problem cooking something... as long as we buy it. But my Aunt's kool though. I'm sure you'll like her."

"Meeting the family huh," says Linda. "Don't you think it's kind of soon for that?"

"Not really," says Jamal. "You already know my parents. And that's because it's business related. You're only meeting my aunt because you lucked out by coming on this trip. So think of it as your lucky day."

*   *   *

Jamal pulls into the driveway and puts the RV in park, then turns off the engine. He then looks at Linda, who's sleeping peacefully, in the passenger seat and starts to analyze her face. He then thinks about what she said earlier about meeting his family. And he thinks about what his response was. And he's right. She is lucky. Jamal looks at her sleeping in the passenger seat. And falls, in love, for her and leans over to Linda and kisses her on her lips. Linda wakes up, somewhat surprised, and wraps her arms around his head; and gives him everything he's asking for in this kiss… but that was just a thought. Jamal snaps out of it and finds himself resting in the driver's seat for a minute. He turns around to see what's going on behind him. More importantly, who's around him. And he sees Emily and Kenny making out in that booth. Jamal turns back around in his chair and says to himself, "What is with that booth." He then looks at Linda, leans over, and puts his hand on her shoulder to wake her up. She doesn't respond. Then he gives her a nudge, and she wakes up.

"Hey," says Jamal. "We're here… at my Aunt's house."

Linda yawns, stretches her arms out, and looks around. "How long was I asleep," Linda asks.

"I don't know," says Jamal. "But it was a while."

Linda turns around and sees Emily sitting at the booth, reading a magazine and Kenny is resting his head, in his arms, at the table.

Jamal unbuckles his seatbelt, stands up out of his seat, stretches, and starts to walk towards the bathroom. And before he completely leaves the cab, he says, "Hey Linda."

She turns around in her seat and looks at Jamal and answers, "Yeah."

As he passes the booth, he points to Kenny and Emily and says, "You missed it. They were just making out."

Then he stops walking and turns his head towards her and says, "Worse than we were." Then he looks at Emily for a brief second, then goes back to walking to the bathroom.

Emily slams the magazine down on the table and says, "No we weren't!"

Kenny lifts his head up saying, "Huh, what?"

Linda then says, unbuckling her seatbelt, "Girl, you ain't got to lie to me."

Then she stands up and makes her way to the back to get herself together, and ready, to meet Jamal's Aunt.

Chapter 18

Jamal knocks on the door and rings the doorbell. After a moment, the door opens and Jamal's Aunt Glenda says, standing in the doorway with her arms wide open, "Hey Jamal!" And she gives Jamal a big hug and a kiss on the cheek. "Come on in."

Jamal and his friends walk inside the house. And one by one, as they entered the house, Jamal introduces everyone to his Aunt. As she brings everyone through the house, she introduced Jamal's friends to her husband who is sitting in the living room, watching TV. Then she leads them in to the kitchen where they all take a seat at the dining room table.

"So, how has the trip on the road been, Jamal?" Aunt Glenda asks.

"It actually turned out to be pretty good," Jamal answers. "I wasn't worried about administering the surveys as much, but, it was more the in between time I was concerned with. And because I'm not by myself, there was a lot of decisions I had to make. Like eating and sleeping arrangements. And I had to put others into consideration when making certain decisions."

Jamal then glances at his friends and says, "And to be honest, I wasn't sure how the chemistry with everyone was going to work out. I go to school with Kenny now, and I've known Emily since high school. And I just met Linda a few days ago. So, it was more of getting everybody together and hoping everyone clicked. And we did. And as it turned out, I didn't expect to have as much fun as I'm having."

"So you know everyone except Linda," Aunt Glenda asked, looking around at everyone.

"Right," Jamal answered.

Glenda studies the group for a second. Then she says, "So you guys paired up? Linda's with you Jamal. And Emily is with Kenny."

"Uuumm, yeah," says Jamal. Not wanting to admit what could have been everyone's plan. "Is it that transparent?"

"Only if you exhume typical "hook-up" behavior when you're around each other in public," says Aunt Glenda. "You're forgetting what I went to school for."

"Yeah, you're right," says Jamal.

"What's that," says Linda joining in the conversation.

"My Aunt is Doctor Aunt Glenda... a Psychologist," says Jamal looking at Linda. "I almost forgot, but it's one of the reasons why I wanted to come here."

"So when do you want me to look at this information you collected," says Aunt Glenda.

"I'm ready to go now if you want," says Jamal.

"I'll tell you what," says Aunt Glenda. "Let's eat first. Then, I'll take the survey and go over the information you've collected. How long did you want my prospectus to be?"

"A couple of pages," says Jamal. "Or however long it turns out to be. I'm not asking for a scientific journal entry or anything but, I just wanted a professional citation to go with it."

"Okay," says Aunt Glenda. "I can do that."

"Ok bet," says Jamal standing up excited. "Let me go get everything."

"Hey Jamal," says Aunt Glenda catching him before he leaves the kitchen. "You guys like barbeque? Cause I got a taste for it."

Chapter 19

Jamal leaves his Aunt's house and is walking down the driveway, on his way to the RV. Along the way, he's fishing for his keys to the RV in his pocket. By the time he reaches the door to the RV, he has his keys in hand. So he unlocks the door, and makes his way inside. Once inside, he goes to the bedroom and stands on the side of the bed. Jamal then leans forward and allows himself to fall across the top of the bed. Jamal then collects himself by taking a deep breath, and then exhaling. He then grabs his book bag, which is on the side of the bed, unzips the main compartment of his book bag and pulls out a pack of cigarillos. The kind that's two for a dollar, and about a gram and a half of weed that's inside a sandwich bag. Jamal zips his book bag back up. And with his weed and pack of cigarillos in hand, he heads to the kitchen.

Once Jamal gets to the kitchen, he grabs the trash can and sits in the booth. And he sits the trash can on the floor next to him. Jamal opens the pack of cigarillos or blunts and pulls out the softest one he found, while squeezing the blunts through the front and back sides of the pack. He then reseals the pack of blunts, to maintain its freshness, and to keep it soft.

Next, he examines the blunt to find the line that goes the entire length of it. Once he found it, he then runs his tongue along the entire line to moisten it. Then, he takes his thumb nail, which isn't that long, and runs it the entire length of the line, carefully splitting the tobacco leaf or blunt. Once he does that, he puts the blunt over the trash can and runs his finger through the blunt. He completely removes the tobacco that's inside the blunt, and dumps it into the trash can.

After that, Jamal sits the now empty blunt on the table and grabs the sandwich bag with the weed in it. Just as he does that, he realizes he can't break the weed down on the bare table, because it could then be difficult to get all of the weed into the blunt. So he grabs one of the marketing papers, from the survey, that's in the box and folds it in half. Then he folds it in half again. He then folds it in half one more time, then opens the paper to keep the second fold. Next, he goes in the sandwich bag and pulls out a few buds, that should be enough to fill the blunt, and sits it on top of the now folded paper. Jamal then begins to break down the buds on top of the folded paper.

Once he's done, he picks up the blunt, wets his lips, both inside and outside, and puts the beginning edge of the blunt, with the line going across it, in his mouth enough to cover the line, and pulls it out. He does this for the entire length of the blunt.

Once he's finished, he takes the end of the folded paper, with the weed in it, places it in the center of the blunt, near the beginning with the line on top, and taps the folded paper, hard enough so the weed slides out, for the entire length of the blunt.

When he's done, he takes his finger and slides it down the center of the fold where the weed was, over the center of the blunt, so the remnants could fall into it with the rest of the weed.

Next, he carefully picks up the blunt, that now has weed in it, and carefully spreads the weed throughout the blunt with his finger. Then, holding the blunt with both hands and using his thumbs, rolls the bottom of the blunt, in the center, over the weed. And he makes sure he tucks it in beneath the line that's on top; pulling the line over and onto the bottom to start the sealing process. And he does that for the entire length of the blunt.

Now, to make sure it stays sealed, he takes the blunt and puts half of it in his mouth, and turns it a few rotations with the seal. Jamal then takes it out of his mouth and does the other half the same way. Now that the blunt or cigarillo is rolled, Jamal cleans up his area by putting the rest of the weed and cigarillo pack, back in his book bag. Then he puts the folded paper back in the box. And puts the trash can back where he got it from.

Now that everything's cleaned and put up, Jamal makes it back to the booth and sits down. He pulls a lighter out of his pocket, picks up the blunt, and puts it in his mouth. Jamal then lights the blunt and takes a deep pull. Then he exhales and starts reflecting on how things are going up to this point and he is satisfied. He's got his surveys pretty much finished. Everyone's getting along well. And he's got his presentation to do, at the conference, in a few days. Everything's good. "I wonder why Aunt Glenda didn't say anything about her cancer," Jamal says to himself. "She must be in remission or something. I don't know. I'll talk to her about it tomorrow." Jamal takes another pull from the blunt, and exhales. Just as Jamal's feeling content with his highness, and getting ready to put the blunt out, the door to the RV opens, and in walks Linda, Emily, and Kenny.

"Oh my god Jamal," says Linda. "I didn't know you smoked."

"Yeah," replies Jamal laughing to himself a little. "I smoke. I've been doin' it this whole time we've been on this trip. I just didn't do it around anyone."

"You're smoking weed, right?" Linda asks.

"Yeah," Jamal answers.

"It smells good," says Linda getting comfortable and sitting next to Jamal.

"Yeah it does," says Emily sitting across from Jamal with Kenny.

"Y'all want in?" Jamal asks passing it to Linda.

"I'll smoke with you, Jamal," says Linda grabbing the blunt from Jamal. "It's been a while since I did this." Linda takes a pull. Then exhales and says, "Don't look at me differently though. I'm not a weed head."

"Neither am I," Jamal responds.

Linda takes another hit and passes it to Kenny who sitting right across from her. Just as he takes it from Linda, Emily asks, "You goin in with them?"

Kenny looks at Emily and says, "Might as well. What's it goin' to hurt." Then he takes a pull.

Emily looks at everyone and gets a little nervous and says, "Well, make sure you pass it to me when you get done."

Kenny takes another hit then passes it to Emily. She looks at it, then looks at Linda and Jamal and they're looking back at her. She picks it up, takes a pull and inhales through her mouth and she starts coughing.

Everyone laughs and she says, "It's not funny. What is this, exotic or something?"

"It's medical grade," says Jamal. "It's the last grade of weed before it becomes exotic, so I guess you can say it's a strong reg."

Emily takes another pull then passes it back to Jamal. Then he says, "Everybody good? Or y'all want another hit before I put it out."

"I'll take another hit," says Linda.

"I'm good for one more hit, too," says Kenny.

"Fine," says Emily. "Make sure you pass it to me, too."

Jamal takes a deep hit and passes it to Linda. Linda grabs the blunt, takes a pull, then asks, "So were you going to stay in here for the rest of the night, or did you plan on coming back in."

Jamal responds, "I was going to come back in. I just wanted to setup everything I need to work on the presentation. So when we came back, I could just get right to it."

"So what about the weed," Linda asks as she passes it to Kenny.

"It's just a part of my process," says Jamal. "I was in the middle of unwinding and trying to get focused."

"So what did you tell my Aunt before y'all left," Jamal asked.

Kenny passes the blunt to Emily. Emily takes the blunt and gives it another pull. This time a deep one. And then she holds her breath for a few seconds, then exhales and gives it to Jamal. Jamal takes it and looks at her, then asks, "You ok?"

Emily clears her throat for a second. Then responds, barely, "I'm Okay." Then clears her throat again. This time coughing a little.

Richard Greene

"Well, after a long day, we weren't sure if you went in for the night," says Linda. "So we told your Aunt we were calling it a night and we came back here."

"I guess we could call it a night," says Jamal thinking to himself. "Let me get started on this presentation first, then I call it a night."

"You mind if I keep you company," Linda asks not wanting to be alone.

"Yeah, that's kool," says Jamal somewhat surprised.

"I'll sit on the other side to give you space," Linda says.

Just as Linda said that, Kenny and Emily slid from out of the booth and made their way to the couch. They started giggling and laughing about an inside joke they got going on, that refers to Linda and Jamal.

Linda then gets up and goes to the back as Jamal starts to pull out his laptop computer and some blank sheets of paper. She comes back with a few magazines and a book in hand. And sits on the side opposite to Jamal and starts reading the magazine.

After a while, as Jamal continues to work on his presentation, Linda folds her arms on the table and lays her head down. After a while, she jumps up, catching herself from falling asleep. She looks at Jamal and he's now on the computer. Linda gets up from the booth, grabs Jamal's hand, and pulls him from out of the booth. She leads him to the back, into the bedroom. And she climbs on to the bed and pulls him onto the bed to lay with her. She turns on her side and grabs his arm. She pulls him in to her so that he's spooning her and wraps his arm around her, across her chest. After a minute, Linda's satisfied with spooning Jamal and she turns around and looks at him in his eyes. Then she kisses him on his lips and they start to make out. In the heat of it all, she pulls

94

him on top of her, between her legs, and she wraps her legs around his waist and pulls his shirt off.

At the table, she turns her head over on her arms and starts drooling. Jamal looks at her and sees that she's sleeping. In the quietness of it all, Jamal turns around to see if Kenny and Emily are asleep. And they are. Kenny is resting his head on Emily's lap. And Emily is laying her head on the arm of the couch.

The computer makes a noise and Jamal turns back around to see what it is. There's a message on the screen, in a square, over top of the work he's working on, that says, "Software finished installing. Click okay to restart computer." Jamal exhales in frustration. Then he says, "Great! Now this damn things goin' to take forever to restart." Jamal's able to save his work. Then he clicks the "Ok" button in the box. Next, on the screen, a rainbow-colored wheel appears and starts spinning. "Here we go," says Jamal sitting back and watching the screen to see how long this is going to take.

After a minute of no change on the screen, Jamal decides to take the time to rest for a minute, while the computer is restarting. So he folds his arms and lays his head on top of them, similar to Linda. And after a minute, he falls asleep.

Chapter 20

Jamal finds himself walking, at night, down a main road for a bit. And he comes across the opening of a development off to the left. He turns left and heads inside the development. The second he walks inside the development, he crosses the street, to the right side, and keeps on walking. Jamal comes to the end of the entrance and is faced with a decision. Does he turn left or right? He looks to the left and the street looks like it goes on forever. Then he looks to the right and it looks like there's a break in the road, off to the left, about a block down the street. To gain a small sense of direction or an idea of where he's at, Jamal looks at the street sign and makes his decision. Jamal decides to go right, down the road called "High St.".

While walking down the street, on his way to the break in the road, Jamal is given the impression that this development is a typical suburban neighborhood or development. With sidewalks and gutters that aren't square but rounded off. Jamal crosses the street and approaches the break in the road, and it's another street. Jamal looks at the street sign and it's green with white lettering that says "Elm St." With nothing to lose and a small sense of curiosity, Jamal turns left and continues down the street called "Elm St."

Linda leaves the bedroom and walks to the common area and stops at the booth. She sees there's a full bottle of water on the table. She takes it and drinks it halfway down. When she pulls the bottle away from her mouth, she notices the couch is empty and the door is wide open. Thinking Emily and Kenny left to go outside, she went outside to find them. When Linda steps foot outside the door, she walks down a few steps and the door slams shut behind her. She turns around and tries to open the door and it's locked. Out of ideas for the moment, Linda sits on the step and tries to figure out what she wants to do. Looking ahead, the only option she's come to is to start walking and see where it goes. And just as she comes to that conclusion, she sees someone walking down the intersecting street to her cul-de-sac. And it is Jamal. Curious as to where he's going, she gets up and decides to go after him before she loses him.

Walking down "Elm St.", Jamal starts to smell the scent of chocolate chip cookies as he approaches an intersecting street called "Market St.". With another decision to make, he smells the air. And with the scent getting stronger to the left, he decides to go left; in search of getting a taste of those chocolate chip cookies.

While walking down "Market St." Jamal looks at some of the houses along the way. And even though some are connected to each other, they sort of take a shape of certain stores. Some have the lights on. Others don't.

Only a few look run down and have the doors boarded up. In the middle of the sidewalk coming up, Jamal notices there's something up there. When Jamal approaches it, he sees there's a big anvil in the middle of the sidewalk. It's about his waist high and has "Acme", in white wet paint, written across it. And on top of it is a tray, sitting on a small table cloth, with an empty bag on it that says "Chocolate Chip Cookies", hand written in purple ink. And next to that, on a white napkin, is a chocolate chip cookie. Feeling accomplished and having his spirits lifted a little, he knows that eating this chocolate chip cookie is inevitable. To Jamal, since he's been in this dream, he feels that his destiny, is to be with this cookie. And eat this cookie.

Just as Jamal puts his hand on the cookie to pick it up, Linda comes around the corner, and sees what's about to take place. Jamal's about to eat a cookie with nothing to drink. Nothing to wash it down with. So she picks up her hustle, and walks a little faster. But as she does it, her feet sort of feel stuck to the ground. And she's running in place, the faster she moves. It's almost similar to being in a pool that's four feet deep and trying to run. So she stops running and walks with a purpose.

Jamal opens his mouth, places the cookie inside, and takes a bite. The cookie is soft. So soft, that there's ridges in the cookie from where his teeth bit into it. And as he is standing there, enjoying his cookie, at the end of the block in front of him, a girl runs across the street. Jamal sees this and starts to put the cookie down on the tray, to go after her. As he does that, a tall glass of water appears on the tray. Jamal drinks the water half way down and finishes the rest of the chocolate chip cookie. Then, he proceeds to go after the girl.

Kenny is walking down the street, at night time, on the sidewalk, in the same development, wearing a pea coat, with his hands in his coat pocket. As he walks down the road on the sidewalk, he says to himself, "Where is everybody?" As he continues to walk down the road, on the sidewalk, he hears footsteps casually walking behind him. So he stops, and it stops, and he turns around. There's nothing there. He starts to say something, but then, he figured he'd be talking to himself. So he says nothing. Kenny turns back around and continues walking. As he continues to walk, so do the footsteps. And he stops and turns around and says, "Who's there!" A simple laugh answers. And suddenly, all the street lights go out, sequentially, on both sides of him. Starting far away. Then one after another as they get close to him. And one by one the darkness gets closer to him. There's one street light that's left. And he's standing under it. There's a buzzing sound coming from the light, sounding like it's about to short out. Kenny looks at the light and says, almost desperate, "... please God." And it goes out. Kenny looks around and the house lights are still on. Including the porch lights. So Kenny decides to go towards the house in front of him and the second he moves, all of the houses with lights on, go out; simultaneously. Next, the moon light goes out. Now Kenny is surrounded in complete darkness. The stars are out, but it's not enough light for Kenny to navigate the darkness. Then, in the middle of the darkness, coming from the same area the footsteps were coming from, what looks like the flames of a torch, is lit. And Kenny sees it. Then come the sound of footsteps. And the flames start to move towards Kenny. Kenny squints his eyes and looks to see if it's just fire, or is someone holding it up. After a second, the footsteps and the fire stop moving. And below the fire, a set of glowing eyes open, like they've been shut this whole time. And it starts running toward Kenny. Kenny screams, turns around, and starts to run; but he can't move. He turns back around to see how far away it is from him. And it's half the distance it was when it started charging towards him. And it's coming towards him very quickly. Kenny screams again, for the last time.

Emily is running along a catwalk, that is several stories in the air, being chased by an unknown creature. She follows the winding path, that'll, looking ahead, eventually lead to an abrupt end. So she starts planning her exit to the catwalk. And at the end of the catwalk, what could be a safe place for her, are two stories below and a few feet across from where she is now. Emily runs and so does the creature. And she makes it to the end of the catwalk and jumps. Just as she jumps, she spins 180 degrees, and faces the creature behind her that's decided to follow her to the next catwalk. Emily then pulls out two Mac 11 machine guns; one for each hand, equipped with a suppressor. She then begins to fire at the creature while she's in mid-air, falling towards the catwalk below. When she hits the ground, she's finds herself lying on a sidewalk, in a suburban neighborhood, with her hands in the air; like she is still holding the Mac 11, with her fingers still squeezing the trigger. When the gun disappears, she squeezes the air, and her hand closed for a brief second.

Emily looks around, picks herself up, and starts to walk along the sidewalk on "High St."

Jamal makes it to the end of the block. And when he looks down the street where the girl went, he was greeted by the lite aroma of weed. And it smelled good to him. Almost hypnotized by the smell, Jamal starts to walk in the direction the weed smell was coming from. And within a few steps, the smell had Jamal being led by his nose. Then with his next step, he leaned into the air, 'cause his feet stopped moving, the aroma picked him up, and he was carried away; lying horizontally in the air with his arms hanging down.

Linda saw this happen. And by the time she made it to the end of the block, he turned left, a few blocks away.

Jamal was in the thick of it. The aroma that carried him for two blocks finally lowered him to his feet. While Jamal was coming around the corner, he saw the same girl go inside a house across the street. And the door was left wide open. Jamal looked at the street sign and he saw that he was back on "High St." So he makes his way across the street and up the stairs leading to the front door. When he got to the top of the stairs, he looked at the mailbox to his right and the number to the address said "420.

While he's standing out there, Linda makes it to the corner of "High St." and sees Jamal looking at the mailbox. Then he goes inside. Linda follows right behind him.

When Jamal goes inside, he walks past the woman with red hair, in a pine green cocktail dress, pointing to the corner in the next room. Then he stops and turns back around to see the woman again; and she's gone. He looks to the right and sees a line of pictures sitting on a thin table, with a glass top, against the wall and also hanging on the wall. And they're all pointing to the same corner in the next room. So Jamal walks in that direction and he sees that the corner is hiding a doorway, with the door wide open. Because the steps go down, Jamal is led to believe that they lead to the basement.

Jamal goes through the doorway and down the steps. Once he gets to the basement, he sees that the basement is empty. And the only light source is a light bulb in the center of the room. Jamal also notices a long shadow of bars, similar to the bars of a jail cell, on the floor in the top right hand corner. When he walks over towards it, he sees a closed door made of bars like a jail cell. Jamal pushes the door to see if it opens and it does. And right behind it is a spider web and a long corridor. Not too keen on spiders or their webs, Jamal looks around for something to help get rid of the spider web and he finds a broom off to the left and uses it clear away the spider web.

Once he clears away the spider web, a door slams shut. And he hears something coming slowly down the steps, making a loud thud on each step. Not wanting to wait to see what it is, Jamal makes his way down the long corridor, that was riddled with spider webs on the top and bottom corners of the corridor. Jamal looks behind him and there was a shadow of something that was just standing there. He turned back around and continued to move forward.

Jamal walks in to a living room, that was sort of dim, and makes his way to the dining room, that was well lit. He sees a woman standing there, talking on the phone, and eating ice cream off an ice cream cone. She stops talking for a minute and looks at Jamal. She sizes him up, starts talking back on the phone, and walks around the island in the middle of the dining room; going into the living room then she disappears.

Jamal then starts checking out the dining room. Against the wall to the right is a tall cabinet set. With a bay on both ends. One side had a three-liter orange soda, half a gallon of vanilla ice cream, a small bowl of sprinkles, an ice cream cone with five scoops of ice cream on it, a bottle of strawberry syrup, and a mirror in the back. The other side had the same thing except instead of strawberry syrup, it was a bottle of chocolate syrup. And instead of orange soda, it was root beer.

Then Jamal looks at the island, in the middle of the room, and it has big bowls of sprinkles, m&m's, and gummy bears on one side. The other side has half gallons of butter pecan, cookies and cream, and metropolitan ice cream. And in the center was a stack of bowls, ice cream cones, two ice cream scoops, and bowl full of spoons.

Jamal makes his way to the center of the island and grabs one of the ice cream scoops and a bowl. As soon as he does that, Linda walks in with a smile on her face and gives Jamal a hug. Then she looks at everything that's in the dining room and her eyes get big. Then she says, "Wow. This is a lot of ice cream. I don't know where to start."

Jamal responds while eating a bowl of ice cream, from the other side of the room, next to the wall with the mirror on it, "The scoops are in the middle of that island."

She grabs the ice cream scoop and heads for the vanilla ice cream in the cabinet bay. When she gets over there, Emily walks in and says looking at everything, "Wow!" Linda then says, "The scoops are in the center of the island."

Then Kenny walks in and sees everybody eating ice cream, and he joins in. After a few moments of being there, Kenny starts to smell something in the air. Then he says to himself looking around, "What is that smell."

Jamal, sitting on a stool, in front of the wall with the mirror on it, sees something in the mirror that grabs his attention. It's a woman in a white cocktail dress with fire-red hair. Jamal stops what he's doing and turns around. She makes eye contact with him, smiles, and goes to him. Buddah Lovaz by Bone Thugs -N- Harmony starts playing. Jamal stands up as she approaches him. She walks up to

Jamal and slides her hands along his jaw and pulls him in for what Jamal thinks is a kiss. And she blows smoke in his mouth when their lips touch. Jamal takes a deep breath in for a second, then exhales.

Linda sees this, gets jealous, and starts thinking of something to pull them apart.

He pulls back, looks her in the eyes and says, "I want to smoke you." She smiles, turns around, and gets close to him so that they're spooning while they're standing and she says, "Turn around." Jamal turns around and there's a joint, the size of a black and mild, in an ash tray next to his bowl that's already lit. Jamal picks it up and turns back around and the woman in the white cocktail dress is gone. So he sits on his stool and starts smoking it. After a minute, Linda signals Jamal to come over to her. He takes one last pull, puts the blunt in the ash tray, and then goes to her.

On his way there, he doesn't trust the situation. So he grabs the three-liter bottle of root beer and takes the cap off. When he gets to her, he takes a drink from the bottle, looking at her. And she says loud enough for everyone to hear, "Don't get too excited or you'll wake up." Then she presents Jamal with an ice cream cone with one scoop of ice cream on it. It's vanilla. Jamal sticks his hand out to receive the ice cream cone and Linda pulls back. Jamal then opens his mouth and Linda feeds him for a second. Then she smears it on the side of his face and she starts laughing at him. Jamal looks at Kenny and the needle to the record player is dragged across the record. And the music stops. He then looks back at Linda and hollers, "FOOD FIIIIIGHT!!!!!"

Then he takes the three-liter bottle of root beer and squeezes it in her direction and it shoots out in her face and gets all over her shirt. Kenny grabs a handful of gummy bears and throws it in Emily's face. And she takes it in the face, unfazed. Next, she's able to get Kenny in a head lock. And she grabs a handful of butter pecan ice cream and smashes it in his face, getting it in his eyes. And she lets him go. When he stands up straight, and wipes the ice cream off his eyes, she throws a handful of sprinkles in his face. He gets mad, disappears, and he wakes up. Jamal grabs the chocolate syrup and makes it past Linda. Linda wipes her eyes, grabs the ice cream cone with five scoops on it, and starts throwing it at Jamal. He blocks it with his arms. She then opens the three-liter of orange soda and pours it on Jamal. Then Jamal feels something hit his back and the back of his neck. Jamal then sees sprinkles fly over him. And he starts to feel something tickling his stomach. Next, before he wakes up, he takes the cap off of the syrup, and flings the syrup on Linda. Doing his best not to laugh and find anything funny, Jamal disappears. And wakes up. The next to go was Emily, after Linda threw a scoop of ice cream at her. And the last one standing was Linda, and she then woke up, too.

Chapter 21

The following morning, Jamal leaves the RV and heads to his Aunt's house. When he gets to the door, he sees that it's been left open. So he opens the screen door and knocks on the front door. It swings open a little more. "Aunt Glenda," says Jamal cautiously. His Aunt comes around the corner and says, "Come in. I left the door open for you and your friends."

"Oh Okay," says Jamal going inside the house. Jamal follows her to the kitchen and Uncle Walt is sitting at the table. He was eating breakfast with her.

"Hi Uncle Walt," says Jamal.

"Good morning Jamal," says Uncle Walt, filled with life; like he's having a good morning. "We have some extra pancakes and eggs over there next to the stove if you want any."

Being a fan of breakfast foods, especially pancakes and eggs, Jamal couldn't turn it down. And from the looks of it, it wasn't a lot. So Jamal figured he could eat them quickly and not be noticeably gone from the RV.

As soon as Jamal was finished his breakfast, still sitting at the table, he came right out with it.

"Aunt Glenda," says Jamal.

"Yes," Aunt Glenda replied.

"I came here to let you guys know we were going to head out for a couple of days," says Jamal. "So I could get a few more surveys done. And more importantly, get this presentation together for this conference on Friday."

"Oh Okay," says Aunt Glenda. "So the prospectus you want me to do, is it going to be a part of your presentation or is it something separate."

"It's going to be a part of the presentation," says Jamal. "There's going to be a section where I cite your prospectus to give us credibility. And I don't have to have it now. I'm going to plug it in when the presentation is finished."

"Okay," says Aunt Glenda. "It seems like you know what you're doing."

"I do," Jamal responds. "Before I head out, I wanted to ask you about something real quick."

"Go ahead," says Aunt Glenda.

"Where are you with your battle with breast cancer," Jamal asks humbly. "The last I heard my mom say something about it, you were supposed to be in the last stages of chemotherapy. And that was a little over a month ago."

Aunt Glenda looks at Uncle Walt, and they both smile at each other. "I'm glad you asked," says Aunt Glenda positively. "It's going on week two that I've been in remission. And I think we've been able to get rid of it."

"Wait," says Jamal looking a bit confused. "Remission means it's gone, right?"

"Almost," says Aunt Glenda happily. "It means that there hasn't been any activity of the cancer since it's been removed. It's still early but I think I've been cured of it. I'm tryin' to stay positive about it."

"Well that's good to hear," says Jamal standing up from the table and walking to the sink, with the plate and fork in hand. "I honestly didn't know what to think, when you didn't say anything about it yesterday."

"Well, I don't go around tellin' everybody my business, Jamal," says Aunt Glenda. "You know I don't like pity parties and feeling sorry for myself."

"I guess it's good that you have your own practice then," says Jamal rinsing the syrup off the plate. Partially washing it. "You don't have to have everyone in your business."

"That's one of the perks of being your own boss," says Aunt Glenda. "You don't have to answer to anybody."

"I'll talk to y'all later," says Jamal. "I'll call you when I'm on my way back."

"That's fine," says Aunt Glenda. "Have fun!"

Chapter 22

Jamal walks in to Staples and the first employee he comes across is fixing a display, right by the front door. The employee stands up and greets Jamal, "Welcome to Staples."

"Thanks," Jamal says ready to fire a quick question to the employee. "Copying paper," says Jamal slowing down a bit.

As Jamal is saying this, "copying paper" catches the attention of an associate, with a motive, at the register.

"Uh, third aisle back," says associate semi-confident. "To the left, in the aisle."

"Thanks," says Jamal continuing his stroll through the store. "Third aisle back," says Jamal to himself, walking past the aisles. "One... two... three... and turn." Jamal takes a couple of steps inside the aisle and looks to his left.

"And I'm looking for..." says Jamal searching for the copying paper. "Ah. Here it is."

As Jamal picks up the packet of copying paper from the middle shelf, the associate from the register peeks his head around the corner of the front of the aisle, and looks at Jamal to see what he's doing.

Feeling like someone's watching him, Jamal turns his head to the front of the aisle and the associate is gone. Then the associate speed-walks past the rear of the aisle, pretty happy and confidently.

Jamal then checks the price, and it's reasonable. "But before I commit to it, is there another type," says Jamal looking at the top and bottom shelf. And there is none.

Then he looks to the right of where he just picked up the packet of copying paper, and the shelf has packets of copying paper all the way down to the end of the aisle on the same shelf.

Jamal says surprised, "Well I'll be damned."

Jamal has found everything he needs and goes to the front end to check out. When he gets there, there's two lines going. One has a significantly longer line then the other and Jamal gets in the shortest line of the two.

The Sales Associate, James, sees this and says nothing. But he gets excited because this is a guaranteed win for him. Or at least he thinks. So he starts speeding up the check-out process for the other guests. Practically giving away the items that are giving him a problem by not scanning. And also, asking them "Do you need this? It's not on sale." He then glances a few lanes down to Larry, another Sales Associate at the register, and tries to gauge whether or not his success rate is high on offering the sale. He focuses back on his customer, gives them the receipt, and tells them to have a nice day. Up next is Jamal.

Just as the customer walks away from the cashier, Jamal approaches the counter, and a sales sign is revealed saying "Sale on paper. Buy one, get one free."

"Get the fuck out of here," says Jamal extremely excited.

Taking advantage of the moment for a text book interaction with a guest, Sales Associate James says charismatically with a smile on his face, "Thank you for shopping at Staples." Then he leans over the counter and says, "Did you find everything okay?"

"I didn't know you had a sale on paper," Jamal says excitedly. "I would have grabbed an extra one while I was in the aisle. As a matter of fact..." Jamal looks at the line behind him and the distance from there to the third aisle and says, "I'll be right back."

"Whooaaa," says James, the sales associate. "Where's the fire? We have all the paper you'll ever need, right here."

"Okay," says Jamal relieved. "Let me get that extra packet of paper."

"Ream," says Sales Associate James.

"What?" says Jamal.

"It's called a 'ream' of paper," says Sales Associate James.

"Yeah whatever," says Jamal unconcerned about technicalities.

Next, Jamal puts his red packet of "copying" paper on the counter and immediately following, Sales Associate James places his packet of "multipurpose" paper in front of the red packet of paper.

"Whoa, whoa, whoa," says Jamal with his hand out, stopping the movement. "What the hell is this?"

"It's the paper that's on sale," says Sales Associate James.

"Well what's the difference," says Jamal. "I see that one is blue and the other is red."

Then Jamal reads what's on the packet and says, "This one," says Jamal, pointing to the red packet. "Says 'copy paper'. And the other one says 'multipurpose.'" Then he looks at James, the Sales Associate, and says, "What the hell is multipurpose paper!?"

"Well," James starts. "People are no longer writing and printing on paper anymore. They're drawing works of art on it. You can use it like construction paper and get a pair of scissors and cut-out different shapes. Or you can just draw different shapes on it. The uses for this type of paper are endless."

"What's the difference between the two," Jamal asks.

"Well, the paper, like I said, you can cut it with a pair of scissors...," James starts.

"I don't care about the different uses," says Jamal cutting him off. "Tell me about the paper. What color is it? What does it look like compared to the other one? You know, compare and contrast them."

"... one has a "matte" finish," says James, feeling somewhat defeated. "And the other has a glossy finish to it."

"You got to be kidding me," says Jamal taking a step back and looking behind him to see if anybody else is hearing what he's saying.

"The matte paper," Sales Associate James continues, "is a little thicker than the glossy paper, and it's white. The other is off-white."

"Is that it?" Jamal asks.

"That's it," Sales Associate James answers. This time with eye contact.

Jamal takes a minute to digest all the information that's been given to him. He even picks up both packets of paper to get an idea of the weight and feel of it. And gives it an overall thorough evaluation, by his standards. After a minute, Jamal then delivers his answer.

"I'm going with the "copy" paper," says Jamal confidently.

"Aw, come on, man," says James, the Sales Associate, upset. "Pick the sale! It's free paper!"

"Hey. I looked in the aisle where the paper was and this," says Jamal, showing the packet of paper. "**Ream** of paper was the only one in the aisle," says Jamal defensively. "No other types were there. Not even a space for it on the shelf. If there was, and I saw the sale sign, then I would've committed to it, 'cause I don't mind paying an extra seventy-nine cents for a free ream of paper."

"Fine," says James quietly, while ringing up the paper. "Have it your way... the total is $7.99."

Jamal gives him a ten-dollar bill. James, very lightly, with his pointing finger and thumb, snatches the ten-dollar bill out of Jamal's hand and rings it up at the register. The register drawer opens and Sales Associate James puts the ten-dollar bill in. And then he grabs the change, and closes the drawer. In frustration, James, the Sales Associate, rips the receipt in half, by mistake, when he's trying to rip the receipt from the register. He then rips the bottom half of the receipt from the register.

Next, he calmly reconnects the two halves of the receipt. He tears a piece of clear tape from the tape holder, that's at the register, and uses it to bind the two halves together. Both front and back. Then calmly gives it to Jamal and whispers, "Have a nice day." Jamal takes the bag and the receipt and walks off, looking at Sales Associate James like he's crazy.

Sales Associate James points to the other Sales Associate a few registers down and says loudly, "The bet is still on, Larry! I'll catch up to you in no time! Anybody can sale eight reams of paper!"

"Thank you for shopping at Staples, did you find everything okay?" says Sales Associate James soft and politely to the next customer, like he wasn't just screaming at Sales Associate Larry a few registers down.

The next customer, ignoring his greeting says, "How many reams have you sold?"

James responds, "I've sold two."

Chapter 23

"Thank you for taking our survey," says Jamal handing the couple the marketing brochure. "If you have any further questions, you can call the number that's on the brochure. Or visit the website."

"Okay, we will," says the guest looking through the brochure. "Good luck with your surveys."

"Thanks," says Jamal. "I appreciate it."

As soon as the guests walk off Jamal says, "Aaaannd I'm done."

"Done with what," says Linda.

"I'm good with collecting data," says Jamal gathering papers together and shutting down iPads. "I think I got what I need and I'm about to go and finish this presentation. Why, did you want to finish collecting data? You can if you want," says Jamal handing Linda an iPad.

"No, that's okay," says Linda. "I just thought we'd be out here a little longer. That's all."

"I thought so, too," says Jamal shutting down the printer and unplugging it. "But we're in the home stretch. And there's no point in giving more surveys 'cause in the past hour and a half, we only surveyed five people. And from the looks of it, I don't think a lot of people came to the park today. Unless they're all gathered somewhere else."

"I see your point," says Linda looking at Emily and Kenny talk at the picnic table that's not too far from them. Linda looks at Jamal and says, "Do you think you'll be taking a break, because me, Emily, and Kenny were going to take a walk around the park. And depending on where we're at, I'll come back and get you or something."

"Um, I'm not sure," says Jamal standing up from folding the legs on one of the tables. "If I do take a break, it'll probably be a smoke break or something. Maybe a quick fifteen minutes so I can get some air. But, we'll see how things work out." Jamal goes back to breaking down the table.

"Okay," says Linda slowly walking off, watching Jamal work. "I'll see you when we get back."

"Okay," says Jamal carrying a box inside the RV. "I'll be right here," says Jamal shouting from inside the RV.

Linda makes it over to Emily and Kenny.

"So Jamal is staying here?" Emily asks Linda.

"Yeah," says Linda responding. "He's pretty adamant about finishing this presentation."

"Girl, can you blame him?" says Emily standing up from the picnic table. "He's giving a presentation, at a conference. Enough said."

"I guess you're right," says Linda. "Y'all ready?"

"Yeah," says Kenny standing up from the picnic table.

"Okay then," says Emily. "Let's go."

Linda, Emily, and Kenny start their journey through the park. Once they leave the parking lot and pass by the pavilions, they come across a path that leads into the trees. So they follow it.

*   *   *

Within fifteen yards of the entrance, they come to a fork in the path. In the fork, there's a few signs on a post. One sign points to the left and says "Frisbee-Golf". And the other signs point to the right, that say "Playground", "Pond", "Pool", and "Park". They take the path that goes to the right. Once they clear the trees, they come to an open field; and the path continues to the right. In the distance, they see the playground and the pool right next to it. They continue to follow the path. And the path leads them to the pool and another fork in the path. This time, the post has two signs that points to the left that say "Pool" and "Playground." And one that points to the right that says "Pond." They then look at each other and Linda asks, "Well, what do y'all want to do?"

"I want to get on the swings, but I also want to check out their pond to see how big it is," says Emily.

"I'm game," says Kenny.

"The pond it is," says Linda.

Then they travel down the path to the right. The path goes into the trees again. While walking down the path, which proves to be a little longer than the last one, the playground made her think of the last time she was at a playground. The last time she was there, she saw potential. And she thinks about what would have happened if she made a move anyway. Regardless of who was with him. Then she thinks about Jamal, and her feelings for him. And what does she want to do.

"Linda," says Kenny.

"Huh," Linda answers, coming back to reality and feeling somewhat lost.

"What do you want to do?" Kenny asks again. "Do you want to go kayaking now, or go sit over there at the benches?"

Linda looks around and they're at the pond. And it's pretty and big. "Let's go over to the benches," says Linda. "What time do they close?"

"7:30," says Kenny. "Why?"

"Let's wait for Jamal," says Linda. "I don't want to get in one by myself."

"That's kool," says Kenny.

They then make their way to the benches. Once they're there, they start to take in everything that's happening around them. There's people kayaking in the pond. Ducks are quacking and swimming around in the pond. There are kids playing in the sand, where they're at, that leads to the pond.

In some areas around the pond, there are small gatherings of people. Some are throwing around a frisbee in the areas that have sand, and some are barbecuing. And, there's couples that are there picnicking. The energy and vibes are overwhelmingly welcoming, and peaceful.

"So," says Linda interrupting the peace, "How are you two getting along? And what do you think of the trip so far?"

Emily and Kenny look at each other and start laughing.

"We're getting along fine," Kenny answers. "And I'm having a lot of fun on this trip. But, the real question is, how are you and Jamal getting along? Y'all seem to have grown on each other over the course of this trip."

"I'll answer that question later," says Linda, dodging the question. "But right now, it's not about me. I want to focus on you two. For example, Kenny, we haven't talked much since we been on this trip, and I want to get to know you better."

"True," says Kenny. "You do have a point."

"My first question is, how do you know Jamal," says Linda. "How did you two meet?"

"I met Jamal at school, in a class we had together," says Kenny, doing his best to answer the question. "We had an in-class assignment to do. And we had to work in pairs. And Jamal just so happened to have been sitting by me. So, we paired up."

"Are you two in the same major?" Linda asks.

"No," Kenny replied. "I'm in Business Management and Jamal is in Management Information Systems."

"Are you graduating too?" says Linda.

"No," says Kenny. "He's ahead of me by one semester. He graduates this spring. I graduate in the fall."

"Oh okay," says Linda keeping up with him. "Do you work, too, or are you concentrating on school?"

"I don't work per se, but I be hustlin' oils to try and make ends meet," Kenny answers. "And I've been thinking about diversifying my portfolio and start selling homemade candles, too. There's a big market out there for that, and I'm uh try and get in on it."

"When you say you hustle oils," Linda starts. "Do you mean like the same oils the Muslim people sell? Cause they come in my salon a few times a week, selling those things."

"Yeah," Kenny answers smiling. "The same kind. Except I go for the high-end fragrances for the same price. Do they come off good in your salon?"

"Sometimes they do," says Linda engaged. "But my clients be wantin' to buy a few at a time, 'cause they know they won't see 'em for a while. And they be wantin' to stock up if they smell something they like."

"And they don't hardly come through for them if they want to buy in quantity do they?" says Kenny somewhat assertive. Nearly cutting Linda off.

"Not all the time," says Linda. "They may have two or three of those little bottles on them. But that's about it."

"See, I'm always ready," says Kenny confidently. "I got a car and inventory in the trunk. If they ever wanted more, I'd just pop the trunk and fill the order."

"You're serious," says Linda, somewhat entertained by his passion.

"As a heart-attack," Kenny responds. "I got business cards and everything. Shit, I even do deliveries," says Kenny looking off in the distance.

"Are you Muslim too?" Linda asks. "Or do you just like the hustle?"

"No, I am," says Kenny. "And so is Jamal," says Kenny looking at Linda smiling. "And speak of the devil," Kenny continues. "How are you and Jamal getting along? 'Cause at first, I thought somebody was goin' home early."

"Nooo," says Linda being shy about the question. "We're getting along pretty well... I like him. Well, I like him a lot more than what I thought I would. But he's okay... I like him."

"Do you really like him?" says Kenny. "'Cause I heard y'all had an altercation at the salon and it got pretty ugly."

"You told him about our social disagreement," says Linda somewhat excited, hitting Emily in the shoulder.

"What?" says Emily responding to getting hit in the arm. "It seemed like he already knew about it."

"Well if it means anything, she just filled in the blanks," says Kenny. "Jamal gave me the heads up before y'all got in the RV."

"Well, it's not like any of that matters now," says Linda standing up. "What time is it?"

Kenny looks at his watch and says, "It's six o'clock."

"And where are you going?" says Emily.

"I'm going to go get Jamal," says Linda. "I want to go in the water in one of those boats before they close."

"Why don't you just call him," says Emily. "And he's probably still working on his presentation. You think he'll really want to go?"

"I don't have his number," says Linda. "And my phone's in the RV. But, yeah, I think he'll do it. I mean, it's not like we get a chance to do this every day. So, I'll be right back... ok?"

"Ok Linda," says Emily. "Don't take forever."

"I won't," says Linda walking off.

"And if he doesn't want to do it, I think you can fit a third person in there," says Emily, still talking to Linda as she walks off. "If not, I'll go in it with you."

While walking on that path, on her way back to the RV, Linda thinks about Jamal and how everything's been going with them. And it's been going great. She loves spending time with him. And the more she spends time with him, the more she falls in love with him. She even gets turned on when he starts showing his knowledge in different areas that she's oblivious to. Like reprogramming the software and having an understanding about the different ways people learn. It's almost like he wrote the book on it.

Linda stops walking for a second, and the wheels start turning in her head. She then gets an idea. And in that moment, her motive for going to get Jamal changes.

Linda continues walking. And before she knows it, she's back at the beginning of the path, at the parking lot.

Chapter 24

Linda continues the walk, and she makes it to the RV. Right outside of the RV, sitting on the curb is Jamal smoking a blunt. She goes over to him and when she approaches he says, "You have great timing. I just got out here."

"How's everything coming with your presentation?" Linda asks while she's sitting down next to him.

"It's not bad," says Jamal blowing out smoke. "I just feel like I should be at my Aunt's house doing this presentation cause I'm at that part where I insert her information. And, I want to be able to deliver it the best way possible. I mean, I know all I'm really doin' when it comes to her part is cutting and pasting but, comradery beats being solo any day."

Jamal passes Linda the blunt and she takes a pull. "I mean, would you guys be ready to go and head back over there," Jamal asks.

"Well," says Linda, "I came to you because they have kayaks at the pond. And I wanted to know if you wanted to go kayaking with me because I think they only fit two per boat."

"Babe," says Jamal, "I'm still not done with the presentation..."

"I know," says Linda cutting-off Jamal and passing him back the blunt, "But they close at 7:30 and it's about a five-minute walk from here."

Jamal sighs and takes a pull. "What time is it," says Jamal.

"I don't know," says Linda getting up. "Let me go see."

Linda walks over to the RV and just as she steps inside, she turns her head and looks at Jamal. And she thinks to herself, "He doesn't even know what he's got comin' to him." Then she goes inside.

Once she's inside the RV, Linda looks for her phone inside her purse and she finds it. It's 6:20. Then she goes to her bag that's in the room and looks inside. "Damn," she says feeling somewhat defeated because she can't find a big enough shirt. Then she turns around to see what else she could find and starts looking around. Her eyes then land on the bed and she gets an idea. Next, she kicks off her shoes, pulls off her socks, and then starts taking off her jeans and her panties.

Jamal is sitting on the curb, thinking about calling his Aunt and leaving. He takes a pull from his blunt, and blows out the smoke. He then looks at it and thinks about putting it out after his next pull. Then he thinks about kayaking in the pond. He then comes to a decision to give his Aunt a call, before he goes kayaking, to let her know he's on his way back at eight o'clock.

Linda comes out of the RV with a sheet wrapped around her and makes a B-Line straight to Jamal. When she gets to him she says, "It's 6:25." And without hesitation, she kisses Jamal on his lips, passionately. Sucking his lips and his tongue when he stuck it out. Jamal puts the blunt down on the grass an arm's length away from him. She pushes his chest and he leans back. And now he's lying on the grass. She lifts his shirt and starts kissing his stomach. Then she licks his nipples and starts sucking on them. Next she grabs his dick, through his clothes, to see if he's hard. And he is. And she starts massaging it some. Linda then unbuttons his pants and pulls them down some, to his knees. She then gets on top of him and grabs his dick. She rubs it on her clitoris some, and plays with it in the opening of her vagina; and his dick gets wet. She then lets his dick slide into her and she lets out moan. Next he grabs her ass.

Jamal then says, "Oh my God, you're so wet."

Then Linda immediately responds, "My pussy's been marinating since we arrived at your Aunt's house. Does it feel good?"

"Damn right it does," says Jamal trying to keep himself from busting a nut. "You got some good pussy. I'm about to cum."

Linda then opens the sheet, lifts her shirt, and exposes her breasts. Jamal leans up and sucks on her breast. Linda starts moving her hips back and forward. And as she moved them forward a second time, Jamal, with his hands still on her ass, squeezed her ass and says, barely, "I'm about to...", and he cums inside of her. Linda looks at him, deep in his eyes, and smiles. Then she kisses him on his lips and gets up. She then says, "Babe, pull your pants up. I think someone's coming." Jamal pulls his pants up, buttons it, then sits up and grabs the blunt. He takes a hit, then puts it out.

Linda goes inside the RV for a minute and comes out with her clothes on and says, "You ready?"

Jamal answers without a clue, "For what?"

"To go kayaking," says Linda holding her hand out for him to take.

"Fuck, I forgot," says Jamal standing up. "Let me give my Aunt a call before we go."

"It's 6:35," says Linda in a hurry. "Can you call her when we get back, pleeease?"

Jamal sighs and says, "I guess I can do that. Let me lock this door real quick." Jamal goes to the door of the RV and locks it. Then he grabs her hand and says, "Let's go kayaking."

Jamal and Linda leave the parking lot and start their journey down the path that will eventually lead them to the pond.

Chapter 25

Jamal and his friends make it back to the RV after spending some time at the pond.

"I can't believe y'all fell in the water," says Jamal opening the door to the RV.

"Don't act like you ain't fall in, too," says Kenny following Emily inside the RV.

"Yeah," says Jamal walking in the RV behind Linda. "And that's because I was tryin to pull y'all asses out of the water. And you had a nerve to make fun of me because I wanted to take my shoes and socks off before I got in the water."

"I tell you what, though," says Kenny sitting on the couch. "I never seen a bunch of life-guards in a panic like that before."

"All that kickin' and screaming yo ass was doin' in the water, ain't help either," says Jamal walking to the bedroom. "I'm just glad I brought a change of clothes."

Jamal sits on the bed and tries to collect himself from the events that took place not too long ago. Then he goes in his bag to pull out some fresh clothes. Linda walks in and sits on the bed behind Jamal on her knees and hugs Jamal from behind saying, "Jamal." Then she starts kissing him on his neck.

"Yeah, what's up?," says Jamal paying Linda attention.

"I was wondering if, instead of goin' to your aunt's house tonight, and hear me out. Would you stay with me and we go there in the morning," says Linda with her hands underneath his shirt, running her fingers slowly up and down his back. And kissing his back. Then holding him.

"Babe," says Jamal softly as he turns around to face her. "You know I got this presentation to finish. And she's got the rest of the data."

"I know," says Linda. "But we're having such a good time. Why don't we just finish the night out here, then head over there tomorrow morning. That's what you was going to do anyway."

"Well what's wrong with doing this over there," says Jamal making a point.

"We're not in her driveway," says Linda, also making a point.

"I tell you what," says Jamal with his clothes in his hands. "I'm going to go change, and I'll let you know what I'm going to do when I get done."

"Okay," says Linda smiling, lying down in the bed.

Jamal then goes to the bathroom to change his clothes. While he's in there, he thinks about the progress they made, as a group, with getting to know each other. And how close everyone has gotten over the past few days.

Halfway through getting dressed, he also thinks about standing on that stage, with potentially hundreds of people, watching him give the presentation. Then he thinks to himself, "I've got to be ready." And then he stares off for a moment. Then he snaps out of it, and finishes getting dressed.

When Jamal is finished, he makes his way out of the bathroom and notices everyone's in the front part of the RV, talking and hanging around the cab. He goes to the bedroom, picks up his cell phone, and calls his aunt. She answers the phone, "Hello."

"Hey Aunt Glenda. It's Jamal," says Jamal with a smile on his face.

"Oh, hey Jamal," says Aunt Glenda. "You callin' to check on the report?"

"No," says Jamal laughing a little. "I know I said I was going to be gone for a couple of days but I finished my presentation a lot sooner than I thought I was. And I wanted to know if it was okay to come by tomorrow morning."

"Yeah, that's fine," Aunt Glenda answers.

"I would have came by tonight, but popular opinion says stay out and have fun," says Jamal not feeling like having fun.

"Well, you should have fun if you're done with your work," says Aunt Glenda.

"I know," says Jamal. "But I'd rather finish everything all in one shot, instead of doin' a little here, doin' a little there."

"I see wha-... what," says Aunt Glenda. Then she clears her throat, and tries again. "I see what you mean," says Aunt Glenda finally. "I'm the same way."

"What's wrong," Jamal asks somewhat concerned.

"Nothing," says Aunt Glenda, trying not to faint. "I just lost my breath and got hot all of a sudden."

Sweat starts to form on her brow. She wipes it off with her hand and notices her skin is feeling a little clammy. And then her hand starts to shake. Then she continues, "I tell you what. When you come over in the morning, instead of just giving you the prospectus, we can finish your presentation together. That way, all your questions can be answered. And nothing will get lost in translation."

"That'll be cool," says Jamal somewhat excited. "And then I'll do a dry run of my presentation and you can tell me what you think."

"Of course," says Aunt Glenda holding on. "And you'll have friends and family here to let you know how you did."

"Okay," says Jamal feeling good about the plans they just laid out. "Well, let me get out of here and go hang out, and I'll see you in the morning. You want me to call before I leave to let you know I'm on the way?"

"Yeah, so I can be ready for you all," says Aunt Glenda.

"Okay, I'll talk to you later," says Jamal.

"Ok then," Aunt Glenda responds. "Bye bye."

"Bye," says Jamal.

As soon as Aunt Glenda hangs up the phone, she falls to the floor and makes a loud boom. This sound made her husband, Uncle Walt, rush to the kitchen to where she was to see if she was okay. When he got to her, she was unconscious.

Chapter 26

Jamal wakes up the next day in bed, and Linda is lying on his chest, with her arm across him; asleep, with a shirt on. Jamal slides from underneath her and reaches down on the floor, in his pants pocket, and pulls out his phone; and looks at the time. It's 9:30. That's already too late for him. So he eases his way out of the bed, trying not to wake up Linda, and puts on his pants. Then he walks quietly through the RV to the side door to go outside. And he stops to look at Emily and Kenny. And they're lying together, asleep, on the futon. Jamal shakes his head, laughs to himself, and opens the door to go outside. Once Jamal is outside, he calls his aunt to let her know he's on his way. But she doesn't answer. He waits another five minutes and calls again, but still no answer. So he leaves a message on her cell phone.

"Hey Aunt Glenda, it's Jamal," says Jamal. "I was just calling to let you know that I'm on my way. See you when

I get there." Then Jamal ends the call, and heads back inside the RV.

Once Jamal is inside the RV, he makes his way back into the bedroom. When he gets in the bedroom, he sits on the edge of the bed and starts putting his shoes and socks on. While he's doing that, Linda wakes up and sees Jamal and says, "Hey. I see someone's up early."

Jamal replies, "Early? It's 9:40."

Then he ties his shoes, stands up, and makes his way out of the bedroom.

Linda gets up saying, "Wait babe. Where you goin'?"

Jamal hollers back, "I'm goin' to my aunt's house."

"Okay, babe," says Linda getting out of the bed. "I want to go too." Then she starts putting on her clothes.

Jamal starts the RV. Let's it run for a minute. Then pulls off.

When Linda gets dressed, she joins Jamal in the cab by sitting in the passenger seat. On their way to Jamal's aunt's house, Kenny and Emily both wake up and start eating breakfast. They ask Linda if she's hungry and she declines because she wants to wait to eat with Jamal.

After fifteen minutes of being on the road, Jamal makes it to his aunt's house. But as he approaches, he notices there's a few extra cars than normal. So instead of parking in the driveway, he parks in the street, alongside the sidewalk, in front of the house. "I'll be right back," says Jamal. Turning off the engine and unbuckling his seat belt. Jamal leaves the RV and makes his way to the front door. When he gets to the front door, he gives an ambitious knock. Jamal waits a moment, and there's no response. So he knocks again, and the door opens slowly. And standing at the door, with the phone in hand, is his uncle; with a lifeless look on his face.

"Hey Uncle Walt," says Jamal. "Is…"

And before he could finish, his uncle says, "You have impeccable timing. Your mom's on the phone." And hands Jamal the phone. "Come in," says Uncle Walt. Jamal walks in, and Uncle Walt closes the door behind him.

While Jamal is walking through the house, on his way to the kitchen, he notices there's people sitting in the living room, watching TV, that he doesn't know. And they all look at him when he passes by. When he gets to the kitchen, there's someone else in the kitchen that he doesn't know. And she looks at Jamal with an expressionless face, and puts the coffee mug on the table.

"Hello," says Jamal, answering the phone, unsure of what's going on.

"Jamal," says Beverly, on the phone.

"Yeah," he responds.

"There's something I have to talk to you about," says Beverly. "Are you sitting down?"

"Not yet, hold on a sec," says Jamal.

Jamal goes to another room in the house, that no one is in, and sits on the couch.

"Ok mom, go ahead," says Jamal, curious as to what is going on.

"Jamal... Aunt Glenda passed away last night," says Beverly. "We think it was from complications from the breast cancer. But we won't know until we get the autopsy report."

Jamal becomes numb and spiritless.

Nervous as to what he says next, Jamal says carefully, "Wh..., what about the report? The prospectus she was working on."

"She was able to finish it before she passed," says Beverly. "Uncle Walt has it for you. Are you ok?"

"Yeah," says Jamal unsure of himself. "I was just was... What do I do now? When's the funeral?"

"We're working on that now," says Beverly. "But we can't do anything until we get the body to the funeral home."

"What about the prospectus again," Jamal asks. "You said Uncle Walt has it?"

"Yes," Beverly answers. "Just ask him for it and he'll give it to you."

"Okay," says Jamal. "You want to talk back to Uncle Walt?"

"Yes," says Beverly.

"Okay Mom," says Jamal. "Hold on."

"Jamal," Beverly says quickly before he gets off the phone.

"Yes," Jamal answers.

"Good luck at your conference," says Beverly. Jamal smiles a bit. "We're over here cheering for you."

"Thanks Mom," says Jamal humbled. "Hold on."

Jamal walks to the kitchen. On his way there, experiencing some shock and feeling lost, it feels like he's floating through the house. When he makes it to the kitchen, Uncle Walt is in there.

"Here's my mom," says Jamal monotone. And he gives the phone to his uncle.

"And here's the report your Aunt Glenda was working on, that you asked for," says Uncle Walt. "She was able to finish it before she passed."

He hands Jamal a nine by twelve-inch clasp envelope and a CD. Jamal takes it and says, "Thanks."

Next, Jamal heads to the front door. He opens it, and leaves the house. Jamal, in a daze, proceeds to walk across the front yard to the RV. He opens the RV door, and goes inside. The look on his face says it all. Kenny reaches out to Jamal and says, "Is everything alright?"

Jamal walks to the booth, drops the envelope and CD on the table and says, "My aunt passed away last night."

"Oh my God," says Emily shocked.

"Jamal are you alright?" Kenny asks, feeling very concerned.

Jamal, unchanged in his position, snickers and says, "You know the funny thing about that is... I could have been there when it happened." Jamal continues and gets louder, "I could have been there to make sure she was okay! I could have been there to call the ambulance! I COULD HAVE BEEN THERE...but I wasn't. I was off somewhere in my feelings, feeling good, and having fun."

Jamal turns his head, looks at Linda, laughs a little, and turns back around and says, "If I never would have laid up with you, none of this would have happened."

"What?" says Linda getting up from the passenger seat, in disbelief that he just said that. "How could you say that!!??" Linda gets closer to Jamal and says, "I love you Jamal. I would do anything for you."

"Yeah, well if you loved me, you would have made sure I had my shit together instead of us playing house! I asked for one night! ONE," says Jamal holding up his pointing finger. "And I couldn't even get that."

"That's not fair," says Linda. "Jamal, you don't mean that," says Linda reaching out, touching his arm.

Jamal quickly turns around and backs up from Linda and says, "GET OFF ME with your selfish ass." Jamal then storms out of the RV. Kenny goes after him.

"And here I am fallin' for everything she says to me," says Jamal upset, starting to pace. "Gives a fuck about nobody but yourself," Jamal continues, walking in circles, looking for somewhere to go.

"All I wanted to do was spend time with Jamal before he goes to do his presentation," says Linda holding back her tears, trying to defend her actions. "Because once that's over, we're going to go back home and have to deal with the bullshit that goes on there. And he might not have time for me," says Linda upset.

"Girrrrlll," says Emily getting up from the couch. "Get your stuff and let's go. I think they need some space."

Linda starts crying. Emily pushes Linda, and she resists, on her way toward the bedroom to get their things. Emily picks up her bags and hands Linda hers.

Linda takes her bag, looks at Emily and says, "I can't just leave him like this."

"Let's go," says Emily again, pushing Linda out of the bedroom.

And again Linda resists on the way out.

Linda then says, "I have to be there for him."

Jamal walks aimlessly down the street, on the side walk.

Kenny is close behind Jamal and says, "It's okay."

Jamal stops and says with tears in his eyes, "She was my second mom, yo. This shit's not fair."

Then Jamal starts to fall to the ground and Kenny tries to catch him but he slipped through his hands. Jamal starts crying profusely. And In a fit of rage, not able to do anything, Jamal lifts his head back, and hollers to the top of his lungs.

Chapter 27

It's pouring down rain and thunder storming. Linda is looking out of the window, depressed, thinking to herself, "Where did I go wrong?"

Emily puts the last of their bags in the trunk of the taxi and closes it. Then she opens the door to the backseat of the taxi and gets in. The taxi pulls off. Without looking at her, Linda asks Emily, "Do you think Jamal hates me?"

"No," Emily answers confidently. "It seems like this is the first time Jamal has lost someone so close to him like that. I would like to think that anybody, especially a man, who loses a mother figure, would need time to mourn and heal."

"I just wish there was something I could do to help him get through this," says Linda.

"We could be helping right now by taking a break from each other and giving each other space," says Emily. "I mean we have been up in each other's face for almost a week now. I think this is the perfect time to get some air."

"I guess you're right," says Linda. "Hey driver…"

"Yes," the driver answers.

"How far are we from the hotel?" Linda asks.

"It's just down the road here," says the driver. "Another ten, maybe fifteen minutes."

Linda sighs unhappily. "It feels like we been in this car for hours," says Linda impatiently.

"I know," says Emily laughing a little. "She looks at her phone and says, but it's only been about fifteen minutes."

"What time is it?" Linda asks.

"It's 11:15," says Emily. "I figured when we get settled in, there's this buffet close to the hotel that we can get lunch at. Unless you want to just order out."

"I'm not hungry," Linda responds. "I want to just bury my face in a pillow and stay there."

"Linda," says Emily. "We got to get something to eat. We barely ate breakfast. Besides, my stomach told me it was time to eat over an hour ago."

Linda, looking out of the window, says, "I guess I can go then. And keep you company."

Just as she says that, they drive by a shopping center and it has a store called "The Center" with clothes in the display window geared towards Muslims. Linda sees this. And without hesitation, Linda sits up and tells the driver, "Hey! Pull into that shopping center."

The driver responds, looking in the rear-view mirror, "The hotel is at the next light. I'll drop you off there and you can walk over. It's about ten minutes walking time from the hotel."

Linda sits back in her seat somewhat mad and says, "Fine."

*   *   *

Jamal is working on his presentation while sitting in the booth. And there's a lit blunt right next to the computer that Jamal takes a couple of pulls from here and there. And there's also a woman in a satin-brown cocktail dress and fire-red hair sitting next to him, on his right, laying her head on his shoulder.

Kenny asks Jamal, "Are we goin' to give the girls a ride back with us?"

"I'm not worried about that right now," says Jamal. "We'll deal with that when the conference is over."

Kenny then retards his comments for the moment. And thinks of another way to let Jamal know that Linda and Emily are okay, without breaking his period of mourning. A few minutes later, Kenny then says, "I talked to Emily not too long ago, and she said they got a hotel for the night."

Jamal looks away from the computer screen, for a brief second at Kenny, then back to the computer screen, and doesn't respond.

"You know," says Kenny closing the laptop some. "For what it's worth, they didn't know anything about your aunt having breast cancer... hell, neither did I."

"I know," says Jamal responding almost immediately. "And I've thought about that."

The woman sitting next to Jamal, gives Jamal a shotgun. Kenny looks at Jamal and he's giving himself a shotgun. Then he takes one last pull from his blunt, and puts it out. Then the woman sitting next to him disappears.

"I've also thought about, what is it about women having to control everything," says Jamal. "I know they're supposed to be nurturing creatures. But why do they always have to change a perfectly good plan, that's already been established, to fit their needs. It's like the second they see you with a little bit of power over something, here they come trying to manipulate you, so they can have a personal gain for themselves."

"I know," says Kenny putting his laptop to the side and sitting to on the edge of the couch. "I've fallen victim to it too. But that's their nature. And sadly enough, that's what we do to please them. To make them happy. And when we do that, we have to care about them enough to let it happen."

A few moments go by. Then Jamal says, "So you think I should apologize?"

Kenny answers, "I think you should move on, and not hold it against her."

*   *   *

Later on that night, Linda takes a walk over to the shopping center. Once she gets there, she sees that the stores have closed. She then takes a walk over to the store, she wanted to go to earlier, and takes a look in the display window. She sees exactly what she wants to buy when they open. Speaking of which, she goes to the front door and looks at their hours of operation. And she sees that they open at 9:00. Linda smiles with content, and walks away.

Chapter 28

Jamal wakes up to the sound of the alarm going off on his phone. He shuts it off. Then he goes and brushes his teeth and gets dressed in the clothes he had set aside for the conference. Once he gets dressed, he comes from out of the bedroom to the front of the RV. And Kenny sees him and says, "You look sharp bro."

"Thanks," says Jamal, checking himself out. "I've been waitin' to wear this to a formal event or something, but nothing's been coming up."

"It's all good," says Kenny. "At least you were prepared. But uhh, wait 'til you see what I brought with me."

"So you goin' to do it up?" Jamal asks.

"Hey," says Kenny. "Those forums we was goin' to for class, ain't got nothing on what I'm about to wear today. You feel me?" Kenny slaps Jamal's hand and goes to the back to get freshened up and get dressed.

After about fifteen minutes, Kenny comes from the back, stands in front of Jamal, strikes a pose, and doesn't say anything.

Jamal looks up and says, "Damn. You got a three-piece pin-striped suit on, AND you're rockin a kufi..."

"Hey," says Kenny confident. "Go hard, or go home."

"I heard that," says Jamal. "You ready to roll out?"

"Yeah. Let's go," says Kenny walking to the cab and getting in the passenger seat.

Jamal follows right behind him and gets in the driver's seat. They both put their seatbelts on. Jamal starts the RV, and they are on their way to the conference.

*　　　*　　　*

Back at the hotel, Linda and Emily are getting dressed and getting their things together before they leave to checkout and call a cab. On their way to the door Linda says, "Hey, do you mind goin' with me to the store real quick before we leave?"

"Was it the same store from yesterday?" Emily asks.

"Yeah," says Linda.

"How long are you going to be," says Emily.

"In and out," says Linda confidently. "Maybe five minutes... if that."

"Well, when we call the cab," says Emily. "We'll just swing by the store on the way there. I want to make sure we at least get there with enough time to see Jamal give his presentation."

"Have you talked to Kenny yet?" Linda asks.

"No," says Emily. "He said he was going to call me when they got to the convention center. That way, Jamal won't know we're coming."

"Well I hope he doesn't get upset when he sees me," says Linda somewhat concerned.

"If he really likes you," says Emily. "Then it shouldn't matter that you're there. He should be happy to see you either way."

"I guess you're right," says Linda. "Let's go. I'll call the cab when we get downstairs."

Chapter 29

Jamal and Kenny make it to the convention center. And they're able to find parking, towards the back of the parking lot. Which isn't too far from the front.

When Jamal and Kenny exit the RV, they both grab the two boxes that everything came in, and they agreed that Kenny was going to have to come back and get the tables. Then they start to make their way to the entrance of the convention center.

Once they got inside, they followed the signs that pointed them in the direction they are supposed to go in. The signs lead them to the check-in table, right outside the convention center hall. When they go to sign in, Jamal noticed his name had an asterisk around it. And when the lady saw him sign by his name, he was directed to go meet up with the other presenters once they got settled in. The presentation was going to start in a half an hour, and that only gave Jamal enough time to go to his company's station on the floor and do a dry run.

On their way inside the hall, Jamal seen a dolly by the door and decided to use it to help them carry their things to their company's space. Once they got there, without hesitation or a discussion about what needed to be done next, they unloaded the dolly. And Kenny then takes the dolly, and the keys to the RV with him, on his way to the RV. At that point, Jamal stacked the boxes on top of each other, and put the laptop on top. Then he opened the laptop, loaded his presentation, and began practicing one last time.

As soon as Kenny gets to the hallway of the convention center, he calls Emily and she answers almost immediately.

"Hello," says Emily.

"Hey, its Kenny," Kenny responds. "Where you guys at?"

"We just got to the convention center," Emily answers. "Where are you?"

"I'm on my way to the front door," says Kenny. "Can you guys meet me there?"

"Yeah," says Emily. "We're already here."

"Kool," says Kenny. "I'll be there in a few minutes."

"Okay," says Emily. "I'll see you soon then."

"Alright," says Kenny. "Bye."

"Bye," says Emily. She then turns to Linda and says, "He's on his way out here. He said he'll be here in a few minutes."

Home boy continues his hustle down the hallway and eventually makes it to the front door. When he gets there, he doesn't see them immediately. So he continues on and goes outside. When he gets outside, he sees them standing off to the side. Or at least one of them. He sees

Emily and he can't make out who the girl is standing near her, with her back turned to him. When he approaches Emily, to his surprise, the mystery girl standing next to her was Linda. She decided to cover. So he says, "Wow, you covered. Did you have this with you the whole time or did you just get it?"

"No I didn't," says Linda. "There was this Muslim store not too far from here... I thought that since Jamal is Muslim and practicing Islam, if I showed up today covered, wearing this hijab, it would show that I support him. And hopefully it would be enough to show that we're on the same team, as one."

"Okay," says Kenny. "Not a bad move to make. But follow me. I'm on my way back to the RV to get the tables and the cameras so I can cover Jamal's presentation."

"Okay, sir," says Emily. "Lead the way."

Linda and Emily then follow Kenny back to the RV.

*   *   *

When Jamal finished his dry run, he took a step outside the convention hall into the hallway trying to kill time. And when he did, one of the production managers from earlier, spotted him. She walked to him and says, "Excuse me."

Jamal turns around and says, "Yes?"

"You're one of the presenters, right?" she asks.

"Yes I am," says Jamal wondering where this is going. "Why, what's up?"

"Okay," says the production manager. "We ask all the presenters to be inside the auditorium, seated, because we are about to start in ten minutes. Do you have your presentation with you?"

"Yes I do," says Jamal.

"Great," says the production manager. "I'm going to need you to give it to...," she starts. "You know what... Just give it to me and I'll give to the A/V team. I'm on my way over there."

Jamal reaches in his pocket and gives her his flash drive. "How can I get it back when my presentation is over with," Jamal asks concerned.

"The stage hand will meet you at your seat and give it to you when you're done," says the production manager. "If, for whatever reason you don't get it back, you can come back to the A/V Room or Control Room and get it. For now, allow me to show you to your seat and I'll show you how to get there on our way."

"Thanks," says Jamal. "I appreciate it."

"No problem," says the production manager. "Follow me."

"Okay," says Jamal following her. "I didn't catch your name. You are..."

"Nikki," she answers, opening the auditorium doors and walking through them with Jamal right behind her. "You know what... we can cover your presentation if you don't have someone to cover it for you."

"And how much is that goin' to be?" Jamal asks, walking along beside her.

"It's twenty-five dollars," Nikki answers. "Here's the control room," says Nikki walking in the control room and handing one of the crew members Jamal's flash drive.

"Oh, okay," says Jamal looking around. "I don't know why I thought it'd be somewhere else."

"Where do I go to pay for it," says Jamal.

"We charge it to the company you work for," says Nikki looking at his event pass. "But because I like the company you work for. I can give it to you for free."

"Really," says Jamal surprised.

"Yes," Nikki responds.

"Thanks," says Jamal. "Where do I go to pick it up?"

"We'll bring it to you with your flash drive after you do your presentation," says Nikki.

"Can I get a second one free, too," Jamal asks curiously.

"Don't push it," says Nikki. "Your seat is all the way down, just to the left."

"Thanks," says Jamal. And he walks off to his seat.

*   *   *

Kenny, Linda, and Emily are making their way down the hallway, to the conference. Once they get there, Kenny shows them to the registration table, so they can get their event passes and name tags for the event. While they're at the table, they hear the crowd going wild in the auditorium. Then Kenny asks the lady at the registration table, "Did the conference just start? And how much did we miss."

The lady at the table answers, "The conference just started about five minutes ago. If you're looking to go, you haven't missed much."

"Okay," says Kenny. "How long does the conference usually last?"

"It's usually about an hour, hour and a half runtime," says the lady at the table.

"Thank you," says Kenny. Then he turns to Linda and Emily and says, "Follow me. I'll show you where the setup is."

"You know what," says Linda to Kenny. "We got it from here. It's the same setup we've been doing for the surveys, right?"

"Yeah," says Kenny. "The only difference is you've got to put the banner up on the back wall of our section. And there's chairs already there that you can use for that."

"Okay," says Linda. "We got it."

"Yeah," Emily added. "Go cover Jamal's presentation before you miss it. We'll probably be in there after we setup everything."

"Okay," says Kenny picking up the cameras and the camera equipment. "Jamal is the last speaker to go up and present, so you have time. And I'll see you guys in a little bit."

"Ok Kenny," says Linda. "I'll see you later."

Then Kenny rushes off to the auditorium. And the girls make their way to the company's designated space in the hall, following the guide they picked up at the registration table.

*   *   *

When Kenny got inside the auditorium, he had a hard time trying to find a place to setup at first. But once he scanned the room for a space, he saw a bunch of cameras setup with people behind them. To blend in, he made his way over there and setup the equipment right next to them. He was then able to get a program so he could follow the conference. After that, he waited for Jamal to go on.

After about forty-five minutes, Jamal and the company he works for was called to the stage. Kenny started recording, and Linda and Emily made it in time to see Jamal present.

Chapter 30

After Jamal finishes the presentation, he receives a standing ovation and turns the keynote back over to the host. He then makes his way back to his seat. When the host closes out the keynote, the people from the control room gave Jamal back his flash drive and a DVD copy of the presentation. Just as Jamal gets up from his seat and start to leave, his manager and good friend surprises Jamal by meeting him at his seat, before he left the auditorium.

Robert approaches Jamal, sticks his hand out and says, "Great job." Jamal shakes his hand, and Robert continues, "You've done outstanding work with the presentation. I can't wait to go over the data with our psychologists, so we can add a couple of things to the software and make some changes, so we can get out of the stages of beta testing. When you called and asked if you could change the parameters and expand the fields, I knew you were the real deal. The problems you had with the software was put there on purpose, to see if you were willing say, 'You were wrong. This doesn't fit a real world application.' And you did! Come," says Robert as he turns around and follows the crowd out. "It's time to meet the rest of the team." Robert turns back around to Jamal and says, "Oh, and I brought Matt too, just to get him out of the office."

"Dude," says Matt walking alongside Jamal, following behind Robert. "You fuckin kicked ass on that stage."

"Thanks," says Jamal. "You really liked it?"

"Bro, it was like I was at your concert or something," says Matt looking at Jamal. "When it comes to business, most people hate two things: Meetings and getting in front of people. And you did it like a pro.
Oh, and way to invite people to come to our station and give our survey a try. It's goin' to be a fuckin mad house."

"I know," says Jamal. "Hey, did you see some of the girls here."

"It's fuckin' ridiculous," says Matt. "I got two numbers already... you?"

"I didn't have time to talk to anybody," says Jamal. "All I could do was say 'damn' and break my neck every time a good-lookin' chick walked by."

"Well, all that will change," says Matt confidently. "We're going out tonight."

Jamal and Matt follow Robert out of the auditorium to their company's station inside the hall. On their way to their station, they ran into a line and a crowd of people that filled the area and stretched across two company stations. Robert stopped near the end of the line and looked at Jamal and Matt. He then decided to walk around the line to see where it started and said, "Hmm. I wonder where this line goes to."

So they followed him around the line and through the crowd of people. When they got to the front of the line, they saw that the line started at their company's station. When Jamal got to the front, he saw that they expanded the area way beyond what he was going to do. The setup was completely different. And there were some people in the company's station that he hadn't seen before.

"Hey Jamal," says Robert walking behind the table, into the station. "I got a chance to meet Emily and Linda. And they said they helped you with collecting the data from the surveys."

"Hi Jamal," says Emily smiling, as he walked behind the table.

"They did," says Jamal standing next to Robert.

Jamal looked at the end of the station and was curious to know who the girl was that was covered; wearing a hijab, from what he could tell. She finally turned around, and to Jamal's surprise, it was Linda. When she turned around and saw Jamal standing there, she smiled some, and started walking towards Jamal. When she got to Jamal, they both were at a loss for words. She looked at Jamal and said, "Hi."

Then he responded forgetting about everything, "Hey."

"I have to get by you," says Linda.

"Oh, Okay," says Jamal snapping out of it, as he moves out of the way. "My bad."

"The girls told me that there was another person in the group that I hadn't met yet," says Robert looking around. "And I'm going to assume that the guy taking pictures of everything is Kenny."

"Yeah, that's him," says Jamal. "He also helped with the surveys and covered my presentation."

"Great," says Robert as he starts to walk farther down the station. "Let me introduce you to everyone else that's here. Oh, and by the way," says Robert stopping. "We got a couple of rooms at La Quinta that's not too far from here. When you get out of here, just give the lady your ID at the front desk, and she'll give you your keys to the room." Then Robert continues, "Here's Pam, the child psychologist," leading Jamal towards her.

Chapter 31

Later on that night, Jamal and Matt are at Applebee's, sitting at the bar table next to the bar.

"I hope tonight doesn't suck," says Matt. "Those girls I told you about earlier..."

"Yeah, what about them," says Jamal.

"I was able to get one of them to come out and chill with us for the night," says Matt. "She said she was going to bring a friend with her. I told her that was kool 'cause I got one of my best friends with me and nobody should feel left out if we pair up."

A waitress brings two drinks and sets them on the table.

"Yes," says Matt picking up his drink. "It's about time. I started to think you guys forgot about us."

"No," says the waitress laughing. "We're a little backed up behind the bar tonight."

"Backed up," says Matt in disbelief. Then he looks around the restaurant and sees a lot of families sitting here and there at the booths and tables. "I thought this was a family restaurant. I guess everybody decided to get wasted the night I show up here, huh."

The waitress starts to walk away.

"Hey, don't go far," says Matt to the waitress. "I'll be due for another drink in five minutes."

She turns around, smiles and says, "I'll keep my eye on you."

"I bet you will," says Matt to himself, taking a sip of his drink. "But anyway, I told that girl she better not bring anybody that's ugly, and a prude. Our goal tonight is to have fun."

"Speaking of fun," says Jamal sipping his drink. "What happened to Robert? I thought he was coming out tonight."

"Oh he is," Matt responded. "He left for City Walk already. He said he was goin' to eat there. To be honest with you, the only reason I wanted to come here is because I wanted to see where these girls' heads was at before I really started spending money."

Linda then walks in the restaurant and stands by the door.

"Hey Jamal," says Matt. "Isn't that one of your friends from earlier at the conference, working in our station."

Jamal looks and says, "Yeah it is. I'll be right back."

Jamal then gets up from the table and walks over to Linda. When he gets to her, he says very carefully, "Hi."

"Hey," she responds carefully.

"I didn't think you was going to come out," says Jamal.

"I wanted to see you," says Linda.

"Table for two?" the host asks.

"No, it's three," says Linda answering the host. "But we're not ready yet."

"Okay," says the host happily. "Just let me know when you guys are ready."

"I will, thank you," says Linda.

"I'm sorry," says Jamal sincerely.

"I'm sorry too," says Linda sincerely. And then she gives Jamal a hug and holds him. Then she says, "I should have followed your lead and not try to control everything."

"And I shouldn't have said the things I said," says Jamal. "It wasn't your fault... do you forgive me?"

She pulls back and says, "Yes. Can you forgive me?"

"I do," says Jamal, looking at her.

They then give each other a loving kiss and held each other once again.

"Hey, me and Matt got a table over by the bar," says Jamal. "You should come and join us."

Linda looks by the bar, and Matt waves. Then she thinks to herself. "No," says Linda. "You two go have fun. We'll get a booth."

"You sure?" Jamal asks. "There's room over there."

"Yes, Jamal," says Linda smiling. "I'm sure."

"Listen," says Jamal. "We might be leaving here soon to go to City Walk. You want to come with us?"

"I'll ask them when they get here," says Linda looking out of the door behind her.

"Alright," says Jamal. "I'll be sitting over there if you change your mind."

"Okay," says Linda.

Jamal then walks off, and goes back to his table with Matt.

"What did she say," says Matt.

"She said they was going to get a booth," says Jamal. "I told her about City Walk."

"Yeah," says Matt. "Well what did she say about that?"

"She said she would ask them when they get here, which I don't know what's taking them so long," says Jamal looking around.

Matt's phone rings on the table, and he looks at it. "Okay, this is them," says Matt. Then he answers the phone. "Hello," he says. "Yeah I'm here. I'm by the bar." Then he waits for a minute then says, "Okay. I'll flag you guys down when you come in. Bye." He then hangs up the phone and says to Jamal, "Okay they're here. She said they're in the parking lot."

Just as he says that, Kenny and Emily walk in and they see Linda standing by the door. Linda then notifies the host that the rest of her party is here. The host then grabs some menus and shows them to their seats.

When they walk off, two girls walk in looking around the bar for Matt.

Matt then says, "Look dude, there they are." Then he waves his hand in the air to get their attention. And they see him. Next they walk over to the table and sit down across from Matt and Jamal. As they're sitting down Matt introduces the two ladies to Jamal. Next Matt flags their waitress down. And when she arrives, he orders a round of drinks for everyone at the table.

Chapter 32

When the conference was over, they packed up the RV with the two tables they brought to the company's station and headed off back home. On their way back, they stopped at a rest stop to fill the tank back up with gas.

During the long drive back, Jamal and Linda became close again. Completely forgiving each other of the wrongs they did to each other.

When they got back to their home town, Jamal took Linda and Emily back to the salon to drop them off. Before Linda left the RV, Jamal was sure to get her phone number. She then gave him a kiss good-bye and he said, "I'll call you tomorrow." She accepted that, and left the RV, right behind Emily.

Jamal then took the RV back to where he got it from, which was the parking lot behind the bakery. Jamal and

Kenny both parted ways. And as Kenny started to leave he said to Jamal, "I'll see you in class tomorrow."

"Al'ight" says Jamal. "I'll be there."

Kenny then got in his car and drove off.

When Linda made it back home, she sat on her couch and put her bags next to her on the couch and on the floor. She listened to the quietness that filled her home, and appreciated the tranquility therein. A moment later, she pulled out her journal, and began to write in it.

> *"Joy, is the subject*
> *Of this text.*
> *Words filled with life,*
> *Makes my words look colorful,*
> *Like a rainbow.*
> *An open window of*
> *Opportunity,*
> *Is poured on those*
> *That are blessed.*
> *Do they take advantage,*
> *Or do they squander it away.*
> *Love, is the subject of*
> *Peace within me.*
> *Joined by my counterpart,*
> *That celebrates me.*
> *In time,*
> *You will find,*
> *Love, that is just for you.*
> *Once you've earned it.*
> *Joy is life,*
> *Joy is spring,*
> *Joy is me."*

Jamal went to his mother's house. His kids were sitting on the couch in the living room, watching TV. He surprised his kids by standing behind them saying, "Guess who's here!" They both screamed "Daddy!" and ran around the couch to him and gave him a hug. Jamal then says, "You guys want to stay here or do you want to go back home."

"We want to go back home," says Shayla.

Then Jamal says, "What about you Jameir, what do you want to do? You want to stay here?"

Jameir shakes his head, then says, "No."

"Well off we go then," says Jamal.

"I hope you brought my recreational vehicle back in one piece," says Charles, who's sitting in a chair in the corner of the living room.

"I did," says Jamal. "I left a half a tank of gas in it too. So you're good to go whenever you're ready to use it again next year."

"Yeah," says Charles. "That may be true, but, the real truth is how much gas was in the tank when we gave it to you?"

"A full tank," Jamal answers.

"Pay up," says Charles holding his hand out. "That'll be forty dollars please."

"Forty dollars," says Jamal shocked. Jamal sighs, then says, "All I got on me is a twenty."

"I'll take that now," says Charles. "Half now, and you can pay me the rest tomorrow."

Jamal goes in his pocket, pulls out a folded up twenty-dollar bill, and hands it to his father.

Charles then says grabbing the twenty with a smile, "Thank you, son. And I'll be seeing you and the rest of my money tomorrow."

Jamal then goes to his mom, who's sitting in the dining room reading a book and says, "Hey Mom, where are their bags?"

"I'm doing fine Jamal, thanks for asking," says Beverly as she closes her book. Then she gets up and says, "I can't believe you were going to leave us with a half-a-tank of gas in the RV." Then she starts to walk off.

"MOM," says Jamal.

"I'll go get their bags," says Beverly as she walks off.

Jamal then goes to the couch, his kids was just sitting on, and watched TV with them; while he waited for his mom to return.

Chapter 33

A few days later, Jamal walks in to the salon with his kids to get his son's haircut, and his daughter's hair done. When he gets inside, Emily greets him, "Hey Jamal."

"Where's Linda," he asks. "Is she in the back?"

"Yeah," says Emily. "She went to the bathroom."

As soon as she said that, Linda walks in from the back, to the register, drying her hands off. She then sees Jamal standing there and says, "Hey you!" And gives him a hug.

"Hey baby," says Jamal. "And these are my kids."

He then shows Linda his kids. And in that moment, the second she sees his kids, she realizes that Jamal was the man in the park, with the two kids she fell in love with.

Linda starts crying, and gives Jamal a hug. She then pulls away, dries her eyes and says, "Thank you."

"Who me?" Jamal responded.

"No," says Linda going to his son. "Hi, my name is Linda. Is it okay if I cut your hair?"

Jameir shakes his head and says, "Yes."

"Okay," says Linda. "Follow me."

Then Jamal and his daughter, Shayla, go to the waiting area against the window, sits in the chair, and wait for her turn to get her hair done. After, Jameir gets his haircut.

www.ingramcontent.com/pod-product-compliance
Lightning Source LLC
Chambersburg PA
CBHW051920240626
47153CB00004B/1306